He Was Her Boss....

A few orgasms—earth-shattering or not—were not worth playing Russian roulette with her whole life.

"If we're going to be working together," she said, "this thing between us has to end. No candlelit dinners, no late-night phone calls... No sex."

In response, Griffin threw back his head and laughed.

She set her jaw stubbornly. "I'm not joking."

He pulled her toward him so she was standing between his outstretched legs and took her lips in a soul-searing kiss. The kind that almost ended up with him ripping off her clothes and devouring her until she came apart in his arms.

He smiled. "Well then, you let me know how that goes for you."

Dear Reader,

When I first envisioned Griffin Cain, he was no more than the charming second brother in the Cain family. Characters often start like that for me, very one-dimensional. Still, I knew that he would have to become the CEO of the company one day. My critique partner, the fabulous Robyn Dehart, told me early on that he needed a goal beyond wanting to escape the mantle of responsibility. Of course she was right. She usually is. So I decided that this charming, seemingly irresponsible man was secretly involved with an international aid organization, just the kind of thing his father would disapprove of.

Of course, then I had to decide which international aid organization to model his imaginary charity after. My good friend Tracy Wolff suggested Water.org, a charity with which Matt Damon is heavily involved. I did a little research (i.e., wasted hours and hours online). I'm tremendously impressed with Water.org. That's what inspired me to create Hope$_2$O for Griffin.

I hope that a few of you who read this letter will check out Water.org and find out what great work they do. I made a donation in honor of the book and think it would be pretty cool if others did, too. I'll be hosting a fundraiser in February through Water.org. If you want to give, too, you can check out my website or theirs for more information.

As always, I hope you enjoy this book and love Griffin and Sydney like I do!

Emily McKay

EMILY McKAY

ALL HE
REALLY NEEDS

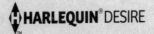 HARLEQUIN® DESIRE

Recycling programs
for this product may
not exist in your area.

ISBN-13: 978-0-373-73226-5

ALL HE REALLY NEEDS

Printed in U.S.A.

Books by Emily McKay

Harlequin Desire

The Tycoon's Temporary Baby #2097
*All He Ever Wanted #2188
*All He Really Needs #2213

Silhouette Desire

Surrogate and Wife #1710
Baby on the Billionaire's Doorstep #1866
Baby Benefits #1902
Tempted Into the Tycoon's Trap #1922
In the Tycoon's Debt #1967
Affair with the Rebel Heiress #1990
Winning It All #2031
    "His Accidental Fiancée"
The Billionaire's Bridal Bid #2051
Seduced: The Unexpected Virgin #2066

*At Cain's Command

Other titles by this author available in ebook format.

EMILY McKAY

has been reading romance novels since she was eleven years old. Her first Harlequin Romance book came free in a box of Hefty garbage bags. She has been reading and loving romance novels ever since. She lives in Texas with her geeky husband, her two kids and too many pets. Her debut novel, *Baby, Be Mine,* was a RITA® Award finalist for Best First Book and Best Short Contemporary. She was also a 2009 *RT Book Reviews* Career Achievement nominee for Series Romance. To learn more, visit her website, www.EmilyMcKay.com.

For the men and women involved with charitable organizations around the world. They give their time, their work and their money to improve the lives of others. They are the real heroes.

One

Griffin Cain certainly knew how to make love to a woman.

This was not the first time that thought had flittered through Sydney Edward's mind. Indeed, it wasn't even the first time today she'd thought it. Oh, the things he did to her body—the decadent, sinful, exquisite things he did.

But that was Griffin all over. Decadent. Sinful. Exquisite.

And so completely, totally opposite from her. Even now—four months into their clandestine relationship—she could hardly believe the things he did to her. The things she let him do to her. No, to be fair, the things she begged him to do.

Begged. Her, Sydney Edwards.

The most staid, conservative, responsible person she knew. And she was putty in his hands. One of which was, even now, tracing enticing swirls across her naked hip.

"I should go," she muttered, attempting to roll away from him.

"No." The sound that emanated from Griffin's throat was low and possessive, more of a growl than a word. His hand slipped over her hip to rest low on her belly as he pulled her back against him. "Not yet."

"I'm already late for work." But even she didn't believe her protestations. Not when his fingers were slipping down into the curls between her legs. Not when her back was automatically arching so that the moist center of her desire tilted toward him.

"Then be late," he grumbled, nipping at her shoulder with his teeth.

They had had sex twice last night and once already this morning. Normally, she didn't stay over at his condo. So, normally, she was back at home, showered and de-Griffined, long before she had a chance to be late for work.

But Griffin had just returned from an overseas trip the night before. He'd had a different trip just prior to that one. In short, lately he'd been gone entirely too much for her taste.

Not that she needed him.

Not that she even really missed *him*.

It was just that…well, she craved his touch. Which was not at all the same thing as missing him.

Sydney knew that her relationship with Griffin was odd. Contrary to her very nature, even.

They spent very little time together outside of bed. In bed, he lavished her body with attention. So much so that she might have worried she'd become addicted to his touch—if she was the kind of person who allowed herself the weakness of having addictions.

Besides, she was twenty-seven. She was young and healthy. It would be unnatural for her not to be attracted to someone like Griffin. She wasn't the least bit worried that she might become too attached. After all, this was Griffin Cain. Charming playboy. Office flirt. The heir to one-third of the Cain fortune. All in all, an unlikely match for her.

So she wasn't worried that, last night, as soon as she'd gotten his text that he'd landed at Houston International Airport, she'd climbed out of bed and come straight to his downtown condo to meet him. And it had been late. So of course she'd bent her personal rule about staying over. No one wanted to drive home at three in the morning.

And she wasn't even particularly worried about her inability to muster anxiety about being late to work.

Still, she tried to fool him, even if she couldn't fool herself.

"It's all well and good for you to be late to work. You're Griffin Cain. Your family owns the company. People will forgive you anything."

"And I just got in from Norway."

"I thought it was Sweden." As if it made a difference. He was always getting back from some exotic location or heading off to some other.

"Your boss isn't even coming in today," Griffin murmured.

His fingers found the nub of her desire, stroking her in a way that made her tremble and ache all over again.

The rational part of her brain lodged a vain protest. She should be stronger than this. She should have some shred of willpower where he was concerned. But she wasn't and she didn't.

Besides, once more wouldn't hurt.

The heat of his erection stroked her moist folds. He was so close. All she had to do was rotate her hips and wiggle to accommodate him from behind. He'd take her fast and hard. One movement from her and they could both have what they needed.

She arched her back, ready to give herself over to her desire, but instead, he rolled her over onto her back. He pinned both her hands over her head with one hand and stroked her folds with the other, making her arch and moan.

"Open your eyes." The gentle tone of his voice didn't make it any less of a command.

She kept her eyes firmly closed, willing his fingers to move more quickly, to push her over the edge.

But he stilled. She knew he was teasing her until she gave him what he wanted. She rocked her hips, bumping against his hand and against the length of his erection. Digging her heels into the mattress, she pushed her hips up, wanting to drive him in.

"Open your eyes," he said again, somehow touching her, teasing her, yet staying out of reach.

She gritted her teeth as she opened her eyes. She wanted to glare at him for forcing her hand, but sexual desire made her languid and weak. Her protestation came out as a groan of satisfaction.

Griffin leaned over her, his usually relaxed smile stretched into a grimace of restraint. He'd teased her, but it had cost him. He was torturing himself, too. It made her smile, that fierce expression—knowing how hard it was for him to restrain himself.

He muttered a curse and plunged into her. She met his every thrust, her gaze on his the whole time, until she felt his control shatter and his own eyes closed. Only then did she let her climax wash over her.

His body was hot and heavy on hers, but the sensation was not unpleasant. She was satisfied. Not just her body but her pride. She may need him, but he needed her just as badly.

He rolled off her and this time, when he pulled her against him, she didn't resist. He was right. Her boss, Dalton Cain, wasn't coming in today. He had had nothing on the schedule today anyway, no meetings to move around, no appointments to jostle. For once, her plate was blessedly bare. No one would miss her.

Even though she was late for work already, even though she still needed to shower and eat before heading in, she let herself fall asleep. Partly because she was exhausted and sated as she rarely had been and partly because her realization brought her a sort of peace.

Griffin should have been exhausted, but he wasn't. Just as he should no longer have the energy to desire Sydney, but he did.

Despite his fatigue, Griffin couldn't sleep. He was still on Norway time. Or was it Sweden? He'd traveled so much recently, he barely knew where he was or where he'd been.

So he did what he always did when he couldn't sleep. He turned on the TV and poured himself a bowl of cereal. The marshmallows in his Lucky Charms were just starting to soften when the doorbell rang. For the life of him, he couldn't guess who it might be.

He opened the door to see his brother, Dalton, standing in the hall. Dalton, who normally looked like he'd wandered straight out of a Brooks Brothers' ad, was dressed in a slightly wrinkled shirt and jeans. Jeans, for Christ's sake. Griffin hadn't even been sure Dalton owned jeans. But there he was. And the poor guy looked worn-out. Like the past few days had beaten the crap out of him and left him in an alley somewhere.

Unsure how else to greet his brother, Griffin said, "Hey, you're up early."

Dalton's gaze drifted from Griffin's bare feet to the pajama bottoms he'd pulled on not five minutes ago before finally landing the cereal bowl on the table in front of the TV.

"I'm not up early," Dalton said drily. "It's nearly noon."

Nearly noon. Crap, he really had kept Sydney here way longer than he should have.

At the thought of Sydney, Griffin's gaze jerked to Dalton. Dalton was her boss. And—as far as they knew—Dalton didn't know that his brother and his assistant were sleeping together. Griffin didn't *think* that Dalton would mind, but hell, what did he know?

Feigning casual, Griffin leaned back to glance at the clock on the TV, then he scoffed. "It's 11:05 a.m. That's not nearly noon. And I just got back from the Middle East last night." Or was it Norway? Or Sweden? Crap.

He could only hope that because he didn't remember where he'd been, Dalton didn't, either. Sweden—or Norway—first for a meeting with Bergen Petro and then down to Yemen for another meeting. No more than a day for each of those trips. Then he'd taken two personal days for a long weekend down to Rwanda. No one from Cain Enterprises knew about Rwanda, but for him it had been the most important part of the trip.

He was secretly involved with an international aid organization called Hope2O. He'd been in Rwanda on behalf of Hope2O working to set up a water district there.

He traveled all over the world for his job. Of course, no one at Cain Enterprises knew he worked with Hope2O. The Cains were allowed to donate to certain charitable organizations, but the family members rarely came into contact with actual poverty. That kind of dirty work was beneath them. To the Cains, compassion was weakness. He didn't want anyone in the family—not even his brother—to know just how "weak" he was.

He walked back toward the sofa. "Hey, you want something to eat?"

"No, thank you." Dalton shut the door and followed him in.

"You want some coffee?" Griffin asked.

"Yes. Please."

Griffin headed for the coffeemaker. Though his condo boasted a gourmet kitchen, mostly it went unused. It was galley-style, open to the living room, outfitted in honed black granite and hickory cabinetry. His housekeeper kept it stocked with the essentials. Coffee, cereal, fresh milk, cold cuts and bread.

He punched a few buttons on his Saeco Espresso machine and let it work its magic. It made a single, perfect cup of coffee at a time, but it was damn slow.

Glancing out into the living room, he saw that Dalton had his elbows propped on his knees and his head in his hands. The guy looked whipped—which was something Griffin would never have thought possible.

Dalton had spent his entire life dancing to their father's tune, and until today, Griffin would have sworn he was fine with it.

Cooper was the opposite. He was Hollister's illegitimate son. He had almost nothing to do with the family at all.

The closest he himself had come to bowing to Hollister's will was accepting the job he currently held at Cain Enterprises. Because Cain Enterprises—a conglomerate of oil, land development and banking—operated mostly in the United States, there wasn't a lot of international marketing to do. It was a cush job. One that Hollister had created solely to lure Griffin to work for him. Hollister liked having his sons firmly under his control. Griffin liked the fat paycheck and the international travel. And he'd never once envied Dalton his position as heir to the family business.

Dalton was the company leader, Cooper was the family outsider and Griffin was just the guy who met everyone's lowest expectations. Until recently, everyone had been happy with that.

A little more than a week ago, Hollister—who was practically on his death bed—had called them all to his side. Apparently news of his impending demise had reached the outside world. Some lover he'd scorned long ago had sent him a nasty anonymous letter informing him that he had a daughter he'd never known. The woman who'd written the letter wanted him to die knowing he'd never find the girl.

A letter like that wasn't something Hollister would take lying down. So, he'd issued a challenge: whichever of his sons found the missing heiress would inherit all of Hollister's wealth. If no one found her, all his money and his share of Cain Enterprises would revert to the state.

Yeah, Griffin was pissed off that their father was trying to manipulate them all like this, but he wasn't particularly worried. The way he saw it, Dalton was highly motivated to find the heiress. He had the most to lose.

If Dalton's weary appearance now was any indication, the search for their long-lost sister was not going well.

As far as Griffin knew, Dalton had been working full-time

the past week to try to find the heiress. That was why he'd texted Sydney that he wouldn't be coming in today.

Ah, crap.

For the first time since Dalton showed up on his doorstep, Griffin considered how Sydney would react if she realized her boss was there. Though they'd been together for four months now, she'd insisted they keep their relationship a secret.

Especially from Dalton.

And here he was about to serve Dalton coffee. As if the machine could read his mind and make coffee, it emitted a series of seductive beeps to indicate Dalton's drink was ready.

Griffin came out of the kitchen and set a mug on the table in front of Dalton. "So," he said, clapping his hands together to hide his nerves. "What brings big brother D to my humble abode in the middle of the day?"

Jesus. Big brother D? Why had he said that? He sounded like a jerk. Thankfully, Dalton didn't seem to notice.

Dalton reached for the coffee. "I think the real question is why you're not at work in the middle of the day."

"Hey, jet lag's a bitch." Suddenly it occurred to him that as long as Sydney didn't come out of the bedroom, he had no reason to be nervous. It wasn't as if Dalton would wander in there on his own. Griffin purposefully stretched his mouth into a salacious grin, just to make sure Dalton knew he wouldn't be welcomed into the condo's private quarters.

As if on cue the shower cranked on in the other room.

"Oh," Dalton said, finally putting together what should have been perfectly obvious.

Griffin glanced at the bedroom door and then back at Dalton. This was the moment of truth.

Sydney took quick, efficient showers. She was efficient about everything except sex. Five minutes max. Another two to dress. Which meant in seven minutes or less, she'd wander out of his bedroom with damp hair, dressed in clothes that had spent the night crumpled on the floor.

Then, one of two things would happen. Dalton would be cool with it, and Sydney would realize their being together just wasn't that big a deal. Or she would freak. And that would mean the end of their relationship. No more enthusiastic welcomes home. No more warm body beside him in bed. No more mindblowing sex. He wasn't willing to give up any of those things.

When he noticed Dalton looking at him, he forced a smile. "Give me a second, will you?"

Dalton nodded. "Take your time."

Griffin crossed the bedroom, made a quick detour through the closet to change clothes and grabbed his keys before heading for the bathroom. Sydney had the hot water cranked all the way up, and steam churned out of the glass-brick shower. The wavy glass distorted the killer curves she normally kept hidden beneath conservative clothes. She wasn't the kind of woman who showed off her body, but she didn't seem to mind being naked, either. He loved watching her shower. Unfortunately, this time it couldn't end with them going back to bed.

Still he couldn't resist propping his shoulder against the doorway of the walk-in shower and enjoying the open sensuality of her movements and the heavy, relaxed, deep breaths she took as she scraped her nails over her scalp. She gave her hair a final rinse and turned off the faucet, reaching for a towel.

As she dabbed the towel over her face, she realized he was watching, and her lips tipped upward in a smile. "Stop it. You know I have to get to work."

"I know."

She wrapped the towel around her chest, tucking the corner in to secure it, and then grabbed a second towel off the rack before edging past him into the bathroom proper.

Even though her smile was relaxed and her words teasing, there was something guarded in her expression. But maybe that was to be expected. She'd made it clear when they first got involved that this was a just-sex kind of relationship. Nothing more. Which was perfect because he was a nothing-more kinda guy.

Still, leaving before his girl even got out of the shower was a little harsh, even for a nothing-more kinda guy.

She bent over at the waist to wrap her shoulder-length auburn hair into one of those turban things only women seemed to be able to manage, then straightened, frowning. "What's up?"

He fished a house key out of his pocket and set it on the bathroom counter beside the contact case and tiny toiletry bag she carried in her purse. "I have to head out. Lock up when you leave?"

Her frown deepened. "Wait. I don't want… I mean, why…"

He didn't give her more time to protest but gave her a quick peck on the lips. "Don't worry. You can give it back to me the next time you see me. Stay as long as you want. There are muffins or you can find something in fridge. Marcella always leaves stuff like that."

"But…" she tried to protest again.

He pretended to misunderstand. There was no point in her getting upset before he knew what Dalton wanted. "Text me later tonight and let me know what your plans are."

She caught up with him just shy of the bedroom door and stopped him with a hand to the arm and an unwavering stare. "What's going on?"

Her stare did him in. Something about her warm brown eyes made it impossible for him to lie to her. "Dalton stopped by. We're going to lunch."

"Dalton? Dalton, my boss?"

He grinned, partly hoping to disarm her and partly because her shock was amusing. "You know any other Daltons?"

"Do you think he's here because he knows about us?"

"No," he said, perfectly honestly. "I think he's here because he's up to his neck in this crap our dad has dumped on him. He may be your boss, but he's also my brother." He dropped another kiss on her mouth. "Don't worry, he'll never know you were here. I'll take care of it."

Then, because he just couldn't resist, he gave her ass a squeeze beneath the towel before leaving the room. She had a great ass. He only hoped that Dalton showing up today hadn't spooked her so badly he never saw it again.

She was going to kill Griffin. What the hell did he mean, *he'd take care of it?* Was he going to take care of it like he took care of that pothos ivy that had been slowly dying in his living room? Or like he took care of… Well, crap, she couldn't even be properly indignant because she couldn't very well rant against his lax attitude toward taking care of things because as far as she knew, he had absolutely no responsibilities in life other than keeping that damn potted plant alive. And he appeared to be failing at that.

For several stunned minutes, Sydney stood there beside the door, listening to the murmur of voices from the other side. She could distinguish none of the words and barely registered the tone. But she tried because somehow it seemed deathly important that she hear every nuance of their conversation.

Which was ridiculous because this probably had nothing to do with her. Dalton had a lot on his plate right now. She knew that better than anyone. She was one of the few people with whom Dalton could even discuss the missing heiress. For the previous week, he'd asked her to hand her normal workload off to someone else on the support staff so that she could devote her time to doing legwork in the search.

She and Griffin had never discussed the missing heiress, but it made perfect sense he'd be worried about it. His livelihood was also at stake. The entire company was at risk. Her job, too, now that she thought about it.

So of course Dalton would need to talk to Griffin. That made perfect sense. Totally, completely logical.

Still, she kept her ear pressed to the door until she heard Dalton and Griffin leaving the apartment. After that, she dressed quickly, barely giving herself time to towel dry her hair and apply a quick, but necessary, coat of mascara before grabbing her purse on her way out. But she stopped short with her hand on the front door of Griffin's apartment.

Crap. The key.

Going back to the bathroom her steps were slower. The key to Griffin's condo sat on the marble countertop, the brass gleaming against the black-veined white marble. She stared at it for a long minute.

"Ugh. Stop being such a wimp. It's just a key."

She grabbed it and stalked to the front door, carefully locking the door before dropping the key into the change pocket of her wallet as she walked down the hall to the elevator. She pointedly did not put it on her key chain. It wasn't that kind of key. She and Griffin didn't have that kind of relationship.

No, they had a very casual, sex-only kind of thing. A no-key-exchange kind of relationship.

She punched the down button with a tad more force than was necessary. She was just being responsible. Like when they'd first started sleeping together and he'd presented her with the test results of his most recent physical, proof that he was drug and disease free. At first, she felt weird about it. Like it was wrong having that kind of information about someone she barely knew—even someone she was sleeping with. Sure, the information was nominally about sex. But there was other information in there, too. She now knew his cholesterol number and that his last tetanus shot was in 2010—from the time he'd gotten snagged with a hook while deep-sea fishing, she'd later learned.

But she hadn't wanted to know about the tetanus shot any more than she'd wanted to know the origin of the tiny scar on the side of his neck. Any more than she'd wanted a key to his apartment.

Which was why, when she got out to her car, she sat there for several minutes, sucking in deep, panic-reducing breaths.

What was she doing?

When was she going to stop fooling herself?

Sex with Griffin was a bad idea. Very bad.

When they'd first started sleeping together, it hadn't seemed like a bad idea. It hadn't even seemed like an idea. More like… an accident. Like when she'd accidently adopted her cat, Grommet. She'd come home to find the poor, malnourished kitten huddled on her front porch to stay out of the rain. She couldn't just leave the pathetic tabby there, so she brought him inside. But he was wormy and sick and even had to have part of his tail amputated. The vet had recommended putting him down instead of taking him to the shelter. A thousand dollars plus weekly allergy shots later and she was the proud owner of the ugliest cat on earth.

Sleeping with Griffin was kind of like that.

Except not at all. Because Griffin wasn't pathetic and he wasn't tame and she most definitely was not allergic to him.

But when it came to adopting Grommet, she hadn't meant to keep him. It was supposed to be just for one night. That's what she'd told herself about Griffin, too.

Last summer, in the middle of a record heat wave, fresh on the heels of an awful breakup with her fiancé, Brady, she'd slept with Griffin.

It was Brady's fault, really. Nine months before their wedding—a date it had taken him two years to agree upon—he'd reconnected with his high school girlfriend on Facebook. He'd apologized profusely for breaking up with Sydney. But how could she feel anything past the burning indignation of finding out the guy she'd been with for six years was in love with another woman? So much in love that he quit his job and moved halfway across the country to be with her, when he hadn't even wanted to sell his condo to move into Sydney's house once they were engaged.

She'd wanted to punch him. It was the first and last time in her twenty-seven years of life that she wanted to do physical violence to another human being.

Instead, she'd calmly emptied the single drawer he'd allotted her in his condo and done the same for the few items he kept at her house. The whole exchange had required only two empty cardboard boxes. She hadn't even had to take a day off work. And she'd told herself she was fine. Fine.

She'd continued being fine right up until the point she'd stumbled onto a Facebook post about Brady's wedding through a mutual friend. Then, all of a sudden, she hadn't been fine anymore. Less than thirty-six hours after Brady married another woman, she did the unthinkable. When she'd run into Griffin Cain in the coffee shop half a block from Cain Enterprises, she'd typed her number into his cell phone. Yes, he'd been flirting with her since she'd hired on at Cain Enterprises. He flirted with everyone. She'd never dreamed she'd be one of his conquests.

Griffin was handsome and charming. With his shaggy, darkblond hair and ocean blue eyes, he looked better suited to professional surfing than international business. His crooked smile and sexy dimples had all the women in the office swooning.

Still, she'd been sure she'd be able to resist him, despite all the times he wandered into Dalton's office and propped his hip on the corner of her desk to flirt with her while he waited for Dalton to come to or from some meeting. Despite the way he'd occasionally bring her gourmet coffee and drop it off at her desk with a salacious wink as he headed for Dalton's office. Despite all that, she knew she could resist him because she knew he treated all the women in the office that way.

And she hated that kind of crap. And she hated people who coasted by on their good looks almost as much as she hated people who got by on their family name. Griffin was the triple-whammy of things she despised in the business world.

Of all the men she knew, he was the guy she was least likely to get romantically involved with. Which was precisely what made him appealing to her after Brady dumped her. She'd been emotionally bruised and battered. When she ran into him that morning at the coffee shop, when he turned on that classic Griffin Cain charm, she did the unthinkable. She decided to sow her own wild oats.

She hadn't really believed she had any wild oats in her. They certainly had never floated to the surface of her psyche before. But Griffin had somehow gotten the damn things to sprout.

The one night she'd planned on allowing herself with Griffin had turned into a weekend. And then into a month. And then into four.

The brief sexual encounter was no longer brief. She'd managed to keep it purely sexual, but it was no longer uncomplicated. A mere call from him had her leaving her house in the middle of the night for a rendezvous. She'd stayed over at his place. Showered in his shower. Missed a morning of work. And now she had a key to his frickin' condo.

It was time to stop fooling herself. She wasn't just having sex with Griffin. She was acting like an addict. And it was time to go cold turkey.

Two

Griffin took a sip of his coffee, looking from the file in front of him to Dalton sitting across the table. He'd coaxed Dalton out of his condo and down the block to his favorite little Argentinean café. Once their coffee had arrived, Dalton had pushed a file folder across the table to him. And then he'd dropped a bomb.

"What do you mean, you're done?" Griffin asked.

"Done." Dalton leaned back against the booth's red vinyl upholstery.

"Like, done? Like, you're not searching for her anymore?"

"Exactly."

"What, you want me to take over?" Hollister expected them to search for the heir separately. But he hadn't expressly ordered them not to work together. "I've got a trip scheduled for next week, but after that—"

"I'm done." Dalton leaned forward. "I'm not looking for her anymore. I'm not jumping through any more of Hollister's damn hoops. I'm out."

"Fine. You need me to handle this, I'll handle it. You know how I feel about Hollister's games. I'll pass on to you whatever I find."

"When I say I'm out, I mean I'm out for good. I'm not searching for the Cain heiress. I don't want Hollister's damn prize. I'm stepping down as CEO. I'm passing the torch to you."

"To me?" Griffin dropped the folder like it had caught fire. "I don't want Cain Enterprises."

"Neither do I."

"Of course you do. This is what you've wanted your whole life. Every—"

"Right. Everything I've ever done has been for Cain and what has it got me? Nothing. So this morning I submitted my resignation."

"You what?" Griffin recoiled from Dalton's words.

"I resigned," Dalton said simply. "I recommended the board name you interim CEO. I can't guarantee they will, but I talked to Hewitt, Sands and Schield personally. I think they'll be able to sway the others. Now—"

"You quit?"

"I resigned." Dalton looked like he might bust out laughing. "Try to keep up."

"You can't quit." Great. His brother finally developed a sense of humor and it turned out to be sick and twisted. "Cain Enterprises needs you. More than ever with Hollister sick."

"I agree. Cain Enterprises needs a strong leader. But you can be that leader just as easily as I can."

And that's where Dalton was dead wrong.

Dalton had been preparing for this job his whole life. Griffin, however, had spent his whole life waiting to take his inheritance and get out of the business. "Even if I wanted to, I'm not prepared to be the CEO. I don't—"

"My assistant knows everything that goes on in the office. If there's anything you don't know, she can bring you up to speed. I know you haven't worked much with Sydney in the past, but she's top-notch. She'll take good care of you."

Shock must have made his esophagus seize because the sip of coffee Griffin had just taken went straight into his lungs, damn near choking him.

"I don't… You can't…" Griffin shook his head. Dalton was stepping down? And he was saying that Sydney would take care of him? The irony was just too much. For years he'd been phoning it in for his job at Cain Enterprises. Just biding his time until he could walk away free and clear. He'd stayed with the company out of duty and because if Hollister knew where his interests really lay, he'd be cut off without a dime. And now, after all this time, Dalton wasn't just giving him more responsibility, he was handing him the entire damn company. "What the hell brought this on? And what on earth are you going to do if you're not the leader of Cain Enterprises?"

"I'm going to win the heart of the woman I love."

Okay. So Dalton had officially gone crazy.

"You're what?" He sat back, waving aside his question. "Never mind," he said darkly. "I know who's to blame for this. Laney."

Dalton's mouth curved into a sappy smile. "Yeah. Laney."

Griffin muttered a curse. "You're throwing away everything for a woman?"

"Laney's not just—"

"Yeah. I'm sure. Laney's delightful. Frickin' wonderful." He leaned forward and tapped the center of the table to emphasize his point. "I've always liked Laney. And even when we were kids I saw that she was special to you. So if you want to be with her, then be with her. But don't throw away everything you've worked for all your life over it."

Dalton shot him a look that was somewhere between annoyed and amused. "I never thought I'd say this, but you sound remarkably like our father."

"God, I hope not." Griffin leaned back and blew out a frustrated sigh. "It's not that I don't want you to be happy, it's just that…"

He had a lot on his plate right now. In the next month alone, he had two trips to Guatemala planned and one more to Africa. The project in Rwanda was at a critical stage and it was the first in that country. On Griffin's most recent visit, he'd made inroads to get the project financed by a local bank, but if he didn't get back down there soon, it might all fall through. The simple truth was, he didn't have time to be CEO.

Griffin set down his coffee cup to see Dalton watching him with that slightly dazed look people in love usually wore. Griffin wanted to leap across the table and strangle some sense into his brother. "Did it ever occur to you that I might have better things to do?"

For nearly a full minute Dalton just stared at him. Then Dalton burst out laughing, and didn't speak for another minute until he stopped. "Better things. Nice one."

Griffin unclenched his jaw. "I'm serious. I just happen to be busy right now."

Dalton took a lazy sip of coffee and shrugged. "There's nothing you do as VP of International Marketing that can't be done by someone else."

That was probably true. His job at Cain required very little. He liked it that way because it left his hours free for his work with Hope2O. And the occasional dalliance with a beautiful woman…such as Sydney.

But Dalton wasn't buying his busy schedule as an excuse, so Griffin changed tactics. "Look, you don't really want to step down at CEO. It's who you are. You're the guy who takes care of business. You're the guy who's going to find this missing heiress."

And until this moment, Griffin had believed that. He hadn't had even a shadow of a doubt that Dalton would find the heiress and, as a result, win the entire Cain fortune as his prize. But he knew his brother. Dalton was fair to a fault. He wouldn't take the money and run. Once Dalton had secured the Cain fortune, he would carefully divide it up among the three—or four—of them. However, if Dalton backed out of things now, then they were all screwed, Griffin included.

Dalton smiled. "Well, it's time for you to step up and become that guy because I'm not him anymore."

The problem was, he wasn't that guy, either. Ever since he was a kid he'd been hiding his true nature from his family.

He was—and this was a direct quote from Hollister—a pansy-assed do-gooder with a heart of gold. That was a hell of an insult to hear at age nine, especially from the father he worshipped like a god.

So—since he was nine—Griffin had been hiding who he was, had been hiding the fact that he cared about the quality of life of other people in the world. Even the people who didn't contribute to Cain Enterprise's bottom line. And he would continue to hide it.

The bleeding-heart liberal born into a Texas oil family. The ugly duckling had nothing on him.

Before now, all he had to do was keep his head down and try to blend in. Now, Dalton expected him to take over. He was going to do the only thing left to do. He would find the heiress. If he controlled his father's fortune, he could walk away from the day-to-day running of the company. He could devote himself full-time to Hope2O or anything else that struck his fancy. In short, he could do whatever the hell he wanted.

By the time Sydney arrived at the office, she'd managed to calm herself down enough to pass for normal. Now more than ever, she wanted to continue impressing Dalton with her competence and trustworthiness.

If her experience with Brady had taught her anything, it was that she had to depend on herself. When it came down to it, she was alone in the world. She had herself and whatever stability her job provided. That was it. She couldn't afford to let herself get distracted by a man again.

Certainly not one of the Cains.

She spent the afternoon at her desk, answering what email of Dalton's she could, and then catching up on the work she'd missed that morning.

It killed her knowing that Dalton and Griffin were out together at lunch, even if she never came up in their conversation. It was a bad omen, like a comet flitting across the sky to herald the impending arrival of a horrible natural disaster.

The two halves of her world were on a collision course and she wasn't sure how to brace herself for impact.

So she should have been relieved when two o'clock rolled around and the door to the office finally creaked open. Hoping Dalton had decided to come in after all, Sydney leaped to her feet, ready to greet her errant boss.

But it wasn't Dalton who walked into the room. It was Griffin.

Her heart thudded and she had to fight the sudden and completely irrational urge to bolt. There were three doors in her office. One led to Dalton's office, another to the conference room. Griffin now blocked the door into the hall, but she could easily flee through the conference room. And, yeah, she knew how ridiculous it was that she wanted to.

But the simple truth was, Griffin wasn't supposed to be part of her work life. He was the stuff of fantasies, and fantasies should have the common courtesy to stay out of the workplace.

As if Griffin knew exactly what was going on in her head, he flashed her a wry smile. He was carrying a thick manila folder and he looked like he'd spent considerable time running his hands through his hair. "Hey."

"Hi." Then she cringed at how breathless she sounded. *Hi* seemed too informal. Too reminiscent of the way she'd greeted him last night when she'd thrown herself into his arms. She tried again, aiming for cool professionalism. "I mean, hello. Can I do something for you?"

He could clearly tell she was flustered because his smile widened. This was just like him. He loved to tease her.

But then his smile faltered as he reached back to close the door to the office. "Did you talk to Dalton before I showed up?"

"No." Something about the way he held himself made her nervous. Like maybe this was more than him just messing with her. "What? Is something wrong?"

"Not wrong exactly…. Have you checked your email?"

"I did when I first got in, but that was a couple of hours ago." Most of the emails that needed her attention came through Dalton's in-box, so she didn't check her own email nearly as often.

"You should check again." He flash a wry smile as he said it, but he looked pained rather than amused—like the one man on the *Titanic* who knew how few lifeboats there were.

Without another word, she pulled up her email on her computer. Ten new emails since she'd last checked. She opened only the one from Dalton. She had to read it twice. And then read it again just to be sure.

Then her eyes found Griffin. "He's resigning?" Then her gaze dropped back to the email and she read it again, sure she'd misread it. *Sure* she had. "He can't resign! This is crazy." Then she looked back at Griffin. "Did you know he was going to do this?"

"Not until lunch."

"He can't resign," she repeated, this time more numbly.

Of course, he could do whatever he wanted. It wasn't like he was legally obligated to come to work. He wasn't a prisoner. But still…Dalton was completely devoted to Cain Enterprises. In the eight months she'd worked with him, he'd worked eighteen-hour days. Weekends. Holidays. Cain Enterprises was his entire life.

"Maybe he's earned it," she said, barely aware she was speaking aloud. And then her eyes saw the tiny detail that they'd glossed over until now. "Wait a second. It says he's recommending you for the position of interim CEO."

"Yeah, that's what he said."

"And that he wants me to retain my current position. So that I can fill you in."

"Yeah. He assured me he was leaving me in good hands."

Her gaze sought his. "He's leaving you in my hands?"

Griffin grinned. "Yeah. Ironic, isn't it?"

Feeling suddenly jittery, she shot to her feet. "No, it's not ironic! It's…" But she couldn't think of the word for what it was.

Unthinkable.

Disastrous.

Humiliating.

Griffin held out a hand as if to ward off her growing panic. "Hey, calm down. This is no big deal."

"No big deal?" Her voice came out a little squeaky and high-pitched. "My boss—the leader of this company—just quit and left me in charge."

"Technically, he left me in charge."

"Oh, really? And what exactly do you know about the day-to-day running of the business?"

"Not much because—"

"Exactly. You don't know much because you're always jaunting off to some exotic location to do 'business.'" She put the bunny ears around the word. But then she immediately felt like a bitch. She was acting horribly. It was just that she didn't like change and she hated having the rug pulled out from under her. She was stressed and scared and she was taking it out on Griffin.

She dropped back into her chair and ran a hand over her face. "I'm sorry. That was…"

"Uncalled for?" he offered helpfully.

"I was going to say really bitchy." She softened her words

with a smile. "I'm sorry. I'm freaking out, but I shouldn't take it out on you."

Griffin crossed over and sat on the corner of her desk, stretching his legs out in front of him. "Hey, it's okay. You're nervous. But don't worry. We'll work it out."

"How're we supposed to work it out? Dalton has left a billion-dollar company in the hands of an overpaid psych major and a playboy." She glanced up at him quickly. "No offense."

"None taken."

"Neither of us is prepared to run this company." But then she broke off and studied Griffin. Really looked at him. Oh, sure. She looked at him all the time. He was her lover. They spent an increasing amount of their spare time together. She'd gone from the point of being in awe of his sheer masculine beauty to being comfortable with his easy grin and smiling eyes. But today she looked at him through a different lens. Today she looked at him as a potential leader.

He'd been raised with wealth and privilege beyond her imagining. He was the second son in a powerful and influential family. But there was the rub. Second son.

She knew from her dealings with Dalton and the other Cains—and from gossip around the office—that the family largely considered Griffin something of a slacker and screwup. Oh, Dalton himself never said that. But everyone knew Griffin had a cushy job. The company paid him insane amounts of money to travel and be charming.

For the first time, she wondered if the cushy job was really the one he wanted.

Cocking her head to the side, taking in his unexpectedly serious expression, she said, "You haven't had a lot of choice before now. You don't want to be CEO, do you?"

Because for all she knew, maybe he did. They never talked about work. Or family, for that matter. Or personal ambitions. Maybe he'd always wanted to be CEO but being Dalton's younger brother had held him back.

Then his face spilt into a grin and he laughed. "Me? CEO?" He shook his head. "No. I've never wanted to be CEO."

She bit down on her lip. "So what is it you do want to do?"

"I want to find the missing heiress. If I do that, all of these problems go away." His blue eyes gleamed with a satisfaction she wasn't used to seeing from him outside of bed.

Which was good—it was nice to see him caring about something, even if it was just finding a way to shirk his familial responsibility. But at the same time, it made what she had to say so much harder.

"You know that isn't actually going to happen, right? Your father has slept with dozens of women. Hundreds. All over the world. Your half sister could be anywhere."

"Not necessarily. My dad's usually pretty careful about the whole birth control thing, so if I operate under the assumption that the woman who got pregnant is someone he was in a relationship with—"

"Wait a minute. That in itself is a huge leap. How do you know your dad was a stickler for birth control?" Even as the question flew out of her mouth, she couldn't believe she was asking it. The absolute last thing she wanted to think about was Griffin's father's sexual habits.

"Where do you think I got my paranoia?" His lips twisted in a faint smile that somehow wasn't. It wasn't an expression she was used to seeing from him. "He drove it into me at an early age."

"And this is going to help how? I mean, you have an illegitimate brother, so obviously he did get a woman pregnant."

"Exactly. But probably not the first time—he's way too much of a control freak to let that happen. I think he'd actually have to be in the middle of an affair with a woman before he ever got sloppy enough to risk her getting pregnant. Which means—"

"Which means the field of hundreds just got narrowed down

to seventy or eighty?" Which still wasn't great odds, but she had to admit it was better than what she'd originally feared.

"More like fifteen or twenty. The old bastard's pretty damn careful about who he lets close to him." His voice was carefully devoid of emotion, but it made her hurt for him in a way she'd never expected to.

After all, she was the orphan in this equation, the one who had grown up with nothing as she was bounced from foster home to foster home. He was the golden boy, the glib son of a billionaire who had never expected anything from him. So why then did she suddenly feel sorry for him?

Not that she could let him see that. Griffin didn't do pity, self or otherwise.

"So you want to find your sister." She dragged herself back to the conversation at hand. "And then what? Saddle her with the CEO job?"

He sighed. "You need vision, Sydney. Work with me here. I find Hollister's missing daughter, I get the money and Dalton is left with nothing. Which isn't going to sit real well with him, no matter what he says. So when I sweep in and offer him a fat CEO salary plus major stock options in the company, he's going to jump at it. Especially if he doesn't have to deal with Dad's BS. I'll put him in charge, let him run things the way he wants to." He dusted his hands together like it was a fait accompli. "Everybody wins."

"It's not always about winning."

"Don't kid yourself, Sydney. It's always about winning. It's only the stakes and the game that change."

Which summed up all the reasons she couldn't be with him anymore. When there was nothing on the line, it was easy to spend time with him and not care about philosophical differences or his lifestyle or the fact that everything really was a game to him.

But now that he was her boss, she couldn't afford to wear those blinders anymore. She couldn't afford to let a few minutes'—okay, a few hours'—satisfaction get in the way of her job. She liked her job, needed her job for the money and the sense of self it gave her. There was no way she was going to become one of those women who slept with the boss, her survival dependent on the whims of a man she had no hope of holding on to.

No, a few orgasms—earth-shattering or not—were not worth playing Russian roulette with her whole life.

"You really think this is going to work?" she asked Griffin.

"It's absolutely going to work. Plus, the good news is Dalton is handing over all his research so far and he thinks he has a lead. So we're golden." He winked at her. "Trust me."

As if. She took a deep breath, blew it out slowly and tried to ignore the fact that she suddenly felt like she was making a deal with the devil. "Fine. I'll help you find your sister. But that's it."

"What do you mean, that's it? That's all I need."

"I mean, if we're going to be working together, if you're going to be my boss, this thing between us has to end. No sex, no candlelit dinners, no late-night phone calls. We—" she waved her finger back and forth between them "—are officially over."

For long seconds, Griffin stared at her like he couldn't quite comprehend what she was saying. Then he did the most amazing thing. He threw back his head and laughed. And laughed. And laughed.

Three

It was cute really, how annoyed she looked.

She set her jaw as bright pink flushed her cheeks. "I'm not joking."

He tried to clamp down on his laughter. He really did. "*I'm* not joking."

"Then stop laughing." As if to give herself a better angle from which to glare at him, she pushed to her feet.

But from his point of view, it only brought her closer. She'd been sitting not far from him but still out of reach. Now he was easily able to lasso her arm and pull her toward him so she stood between his outstretched legs.

"I'm serious," she insisted, but there was no force to her words and—as if she could read his mind—her gaze dropped briefly to his mouth.

"I know you are. That's what makes it cute." He widened his stance and pulled her close enough so that she was pressed against the vee of his legs, the juncture of her thighs against the hard length of his erection.

It felt so good having her there, so right. He inhaled sharply and was immediately hit with the scent of her. Sydney never wore perfume, but she favored a shampoo that smelled like coconut and lime. He was used to the smell of her hair, the way it mixed with the naturally sweet smell of her own skin and made him think of eating pancakes in bed on a perfect, lazy Saturday morning. But today she'd showered at his place and instead of her normal tropical, fruity smell, when he inhaled, he got a hit of Sydney layered under the smell of his own soap. Maybe it shouldn't have been sexy, but it was. He felt it like a punch in the gut. She'd been in his shower mere hours ago. The smell of her only reinforced every instinct he had. She was *his*. Whether she knew it or not, she belonged to him.

Which made her edict that they stop sleeping together all the more funny.

He gave in to the urge to slip his hand along her jaw and to pull her closer.

Her mouth parted and she sucked in a quick breath. Anticipation. But instead of kissing her, he buried his nose in the hair right behind her ear and drew in a deep breath, just taking in the scent of her because he wanted to remember forever how she smelled in that instant. To burn it into his memory.

He felt a little shudder go through her and then he couldn't resist running a trail of kisses up under her ear and across her cheek to her mouth. Then his lips were moving over hers in a soul-searing kiss. The kind that almost ended up with him ripping her clothes off and devouring her until she came apart in his arms.

Unfortunately, he didn't think sex with his assistant would be a very efficient way to spend his first afternoon as CEO. Besides, even with the door closed, there was always the risk they'd be interrupted.

It was a struggle, but he mustered enough restraint to lift his mouth from hers and nudge her hips away from his before he lost all control. For a long moment she just stood there, face tilted up, lips moistened and parted, like she was so dazed she hadn't even realized he was no longer kissing her.

He smiled again, purposefully making light of the irresistible pull she held over him. "Well, then, you let me know how that goes for you."

She blinked. "How what goes?"

"That whole not sleeping together thing you have planned."

The space between her eyebrows furrowed in confusion. Then she backed up a step and jerked her hands away from his hips. "Well, this was hardly a fair test."

"Right, sweetheart." He bopped the tip of her nose with his finger. "Let me know if you devise a fairer test than that. Meanwhile, I'll be in my new office."

He loved seeing her shocked expression as he sauntered into the office that used to be Dalton's and shut the door behind him.

Once he was alone in the room, however, he blew out a long, slow breath.

When it came to running Cain Enterprises, he wasn't nearly as confident as he'd let Sydney believe. He wasn't worried about the day-to-day stuff, but the prospect of dealing with the board damn near had him breaking out in a cold sweat.

The board of directors that Hollister had amassed for Cain Enterprises was a bunch of vultures. If they knew what had happened in the past couple of weeks, they'd be circling for sure. First, Hollister—who had never displayed any sign of weakness to his business opponents—had made a very irrational decision when he'd sent his sons on this quest. The whole company hung in the balance as a result.

And now that Dalton had resigned, from the outside, it had to look like they'd all lost their minds. The board members weren't fools. If they knew how unstable things really were, they'd start swooping down to peck out bits of flesh from what remained of his inheritance.

Right now, the company needed strong leadership more

than anything. The company needed someone who could command respect. Unfortunately, Griffin knew he wasn't that man.

He was all too aware of his limitations as a leader. He lacked his father's cutthroat business tactics and his brother's stolid determination. Perhaps even more importantly, he had no interest in running Cain Enterprises.

At the moment he had two interests: completing his work for Hope2O and the very tempting new assistant that came along with the CEO job. Apparently, being CEO was going to interfere with both of those pursuits. Which was why he had to get this yoke off his neck so he could get back to his real life. He had to find this damn missing heiress.

He dropped into the chair. Testing the springiness of the seat, he rocked back but there was very little give. Damn, even Dalton's chair felt stiff and unyielding, much like his brother was.

Griffin glanced down and saw that the chair was actually the same model as the one in his office down the hall. Thanks to an array of knobs and levers, he could easily adjust it to suit his taste. Instead, he rolled the chair closer to the desk, flipped open the file Dalton had given him and started going over the notes Dalton and Laney had made. He left the chair exactly as it was. He wouldn't be sitting in it long enough to bother changing it.

Sydney stared at the closed door to Dalton's office, trying to squelch the sinking feeling in her gut. Except it wasn't the door to Dalton's office anymore. It was the door to Griffin's office now. This was not good.

Oh, this was *so* not good.

Feigning a calm she didn't feel, she turned back toward the computer at her workstation and mindlessly pulled up her email. If someone came into the office, she wanted it to look like she was busy. And competent. And not sitting here fantasizing about her boss.

Her boss.

Ugh.

She was absolutely not going to be that woman.

Her mother had been that kind of woman. The kind who casually slept with men to get favors from them. As far as she knew, her mother had never strayed into actual prostitution. She'd traded sex for rent, or car care or so her boss would overlook the fact that she was late for the seventeenth time that month. Even if that wasn't real prostitution, it had cast a pall over Sydney's childhood. Poverty, drug use and bad decision-making had dominated her life until she'd been taken away from her mother at the age of six. From there, she'd bounced from foster home to foster home for years before finally settling in at Molly Stanhope's house when she was eleven.

Molly's house had been a haven for the last seven years she was in the foster care system. In fact, Molly was still the closest thing she had to a mother. It was Molly who had been her moral compass since then. It was Molly who would not approve of Sydney sleeping with her boss.

Well, who was she kidding? It's not like Molly would have gushed with approval over Sydney sleeping with Griffin Cain in the first place.

Sleeping with her boss compromised her position in the company. It meant he wouldn't respect her. Her coworkers wouldn't respect her and, worst of all, it destroyed her job security. It threatened not just her heart, but her livelihood.

As far as Sydney was concerned that sort of carelessness was a luxury she couldn't afford. As a product of the foster care system, she had no one to depend on but herself. If the unthinkable happened and she lost her job, she was on her own. There were no loving parents for her to rush back to. There was no safety net. Hell, she didn't even have a kindly uncle who could lend her a couple hundred bucks if she needed it. All she had was her cat, Grommet. And even he was kind of grouchy. If she was lucky, he might deign to curl up on her lap if she bumped the air-conditioning up.

She was completely on her own.

If she lost her job, she could lose her savings. Her house. Even her foster-siblings would feel it, because she'd been helping a couple of them with college tuition.

Just to give herself the kick in the ass she needed, she dug through her purse for her cell phone and scrolled through their numbers. Five of them had sort of stuck together because they'd all been at Molly's at about the same time. She passed over Marco and George. They were both good guys if she needed advice on car care or barbecue, but they'd be useless at this sort of thing. Jen was studying abroad this semester and who knew what time it was in Spain. So Sydney pulled up Tasha's number.

Tasha answered on the third ring. "Hey, what's up?"

"Nothing." Sydney aimed for a breezy tone but landed somewhere near strained. "Just thought I'd call and see how you're doing."

There was a pause of obviously stunned silence. "On a work day? Are you sick?"

"No. Of course not. I'm fine. What, I can't call you just to check in?"

"On a work day?" Suspicion strained Tasha's voice. "I mean, sure, I guess you can. You just never have in the past. Oh, my God, were you fired?"

"No! I mean…" Sydney forced a chuckle. "Calm down. Nothing's wrong. Dalton's not in today, that's all."

Thank goodness she had a handy excuse because apparently Tasha saw right through all her half-truths.

"I just…" Sydney fought the sudden urge to spill the beans. To tell Tasha everything. To share her burdens. Get a second opinion. The problem was, people usually came to her for help, not the other way around. So instead, she asked, "How're your finals going?"

And thankfully Tasha let herself be distracted.

"Ugh. Just awful. Political Theory is knocking me for a loop."

"I thought you liked that one."

And distracting Tasha was easy as that. Fifteen minutes of griping later, Sydney was wrapping up the conversation when Tasha inadvertently delivered the wakeup call Sydney needed.

"I just can't wait for this semester to be over so I can blow off a little steam."

"Just don't do anything too crazy, okay?" Sydney said, that familiar need to protect her sister rising up inside her.

"Don't worry, I won't do anything you wouldn't do."

Tasha's words were like a stab in the gut. If that was the barometer, then Tasha could be in serious trouble.

"Just be safe."

Tasha chuckled. "I know the drill."

"Yeah, I know you do."

"Hey, are you sure you're okay?" Tasha asked her out of the blue.

"Yeah. Great."

"Because you just missed an opportunity to remind me to call you if I needed to."

"Oh. Sorry. You know you can always call. Anytime, day or night."

But of course, Tasha never did call. Like Sydney, Tasha was über-responsible, superpredictable and determined to make a better life for herself than the one fate had handed her. She was also the last of Molly's foster kids Sydney felt really close to. And soon Tasha would graduate from college, get a job and maybe move away. Maybe she wouldn't need Sydney anymore.

Sydney didn't like to admit it to herself, but she still needed Tasha. She still needed to be needed.

She'd known this day was coming. She'd even thought she'd been prepared, back before her boss up and quit, back when her job was stable and her life still made sense. Now? Well, in the past few hours her life had unraveled at an alarming rate. But Griffin was right: panicking wouldn't help anything. What she needed was a plan. Part one: stay out of Griffin's bed. At least until this was all over with. Part two: find the missing heiress.

Of course, both of those things were going to be harder than they sounded. She'd been helping Dalton look for the missing heiress before he'd gone off the deep end. She'd already scoured hospital records and county court records. So far, she'd found diddly.

And then there was the matter of Griffin. If she had any resistance against him at all, she wouldn't be in this mess in the first place.

She didn't need a plan. She needed a miracle.

Four

Miracle or no, she wasn't going to sit around here just waiting for…for what? For Griffin to come out of the office and pounce on her?

She needed a little emotional distance. A way to remind herself that Cain Enterprise's new CEO was now her boss. Not her lover. A way to reestablish the professional footing of the boss/executive assistant relationship.

Her very first boss, for example, had always insisted she call him sir or Mr. Thornton. And she'd never once made out with him at her desk. Never mind that Mr. Thornton was seventy-four, humpbacked and mean-spirited. Still, maybe there was something to this formal professionalism.

Maybe if she just focused on the job, she'd be able to push aside her personal desires. So she did the only thing she knew how to do in a situation like this. She did her job.

She started with the basics. She contacted Marion, Griffin's former assistant, and had her send over his schedule. Marion clearly hadn't heard anything yet from Griffin because she seemed to think the request came from Dalton.

After that, Sydney generated a short action list. Things that had to get done to ease this transition. When Dalton came back, she wanted him to be impressed as hell by how smoothly everything had run in his absence.

She sent everything over to her iPad and marched to the office door, knocking only briefly before letting herself in.

She found Griffin sitting behind Dalton's desk, a file open on the blotter in front of him. He didn't look up when she walked in. His hair—which always looked a little scruffy— was even more disheveled than usual. He held a pencil in his hand, tapping the eraser end against the desk at a frenetic pace. His expression was a mask of intensity and she felt a little shiver go through her. Despite his blasé attitude, he took this very seriously.

Did she know him at all? Sure, she knew many things about him. Like that he had a scar on his neck and that he didn't like chocolate but would eat anything with caramel. And that he watched the *Star Wars* trilogy every year on Christmas. But was knowing all of that stuff the same as really knowing him?

Confused, she automatically took a step backward, intending to sneak out and then knock, but his head snapped up and he saw her standing there, clutching her notes and her iPad in front of her. She was struck again by his expression. By the fierceness of it.

Then his countenance cleared, a smile slipped back onto his lips and he looked like himself again—all easy, laid-back charm. Nevertheless, she was left with the feeling that perhaps the Griffin she was used to seeing was the mask and the intensely focused Griffin was the real man. God, that was an unsettling thought.

"You need something?" he asked, his voice oozing that kind of breezy cool that she'd been aiming for on the phone with Tasha.

"No…I mean, um, yes. But I can come back later. Dalton never minded if I just walked in. Is that okay? If it's not, I can just—" *Stop talking!* she ordered herself. Jeez, she'd never been the type to vomit words when she was nervous. So what was up now? She blew out a breath. This was just another first day with a new boss. Nothing to worry about.

Except, no matter how she sliced it, this was not just another new boss. This was her lover. A man who knew her body intimately. A man who'd driven her to the heights of passion over and over. She'd been vulnerable with him in a way she'd never been able to be with another man. She'd only allowed herself that vulnerability because he wasn't a part of her real life. He was part of her nighttime fantasy world. Now, the two disparate parts of her life were becoming inextricable intertwined and, frankly, it terrified her.

"Sir—" she began, thinking of Mr. Thornton "—just tell me what you expect from me."

Griffin slowly leaned back in his chair, stretching his legs out in front of him and bringing one hand up to stroke his thumb thoughtfully across his mouth, giving her the impression he was trying to hide the fact that he was laughing at her expense.

"Sir, huh?" he asked in a mocking voice.

She ground her teeth. He was definitely enjoying this. "How would you like me to address you?"

A slow smile spread across his face. "I'll think about that and let you know."

"Shall I come back later?"

"It's fine. Come in whenever you want."

"I can knock first. Next time I'll just knock first." Again with the babbling! What was wrong with her?

"Whatever makes you comfortable."

Humph. If only that were possible.

She flipped open the cover of her iPad, causing it to flicker awake and reveal the page of notes she'd made at her desk.

"First off, sir, there are—"

"Okay, I've thought about it. Stop calling me sir."

She gritted her teeth, swallowed and tried again for the formal professionalism. "Whatever you wish, Mr. Cain."

As if he was purposefully baiting her—and he probably was—his smile broadened. "I'd like you to call me Griffin."

"Fine. There are some things we should go over to ease the transition."

"Okay. Hit me."

He flashed her another one of those amused smiles and she cringed. She wished now that she hadn't made such a big deal about the name thing. Instead of impressing him with her efficiency and professionalism, she was acting like a total dork. "First off, I'd, um…like to go over Dalton's schedule for the week."

"I thought Dalton had been focusing on finding our sister."

"He was, but he still had to run the company." She looked down at the calendar app. "The weekly officers' meetings and the—"

"But," Griffin interrupted her, "I don't have to be able to do everything Dalton did. No one's going to expect that of me. At least not at first—and maybe never."

Sydney had to swallow a laugh. He was right, of course; everyone would expect less of him because of his reputation as a dilettante and playboy.

As if he could read her mind, he flashed her one of his charming grins and gestured modestly to his chest. "*I* wouldn't even have this job if it wasn't for my family connections. So nobody is going to expect much. Everyone knows I'll need help, especially these first few weeks. I can hand off most of the daily running of the company to someone else while I focus on finding the heiress. Once we find her, the pressure will let up a bit."

She'd only been thinking about Dalton's resignation in terms of how it would affect her. She hadn't skipped ahead yet to the broader ramifications of how it would affect the whole company. When she did think about it, it terrified her. Cain Enterprises was a billion-dollar company. It employed countless people. He'd not only thought about all those ramifications, but also had thought of them quickly enough to start working on a plan.

She nodded. "Okay. In that case, shall I arrange a meeting between you and…" She let her words trail off as she waited for him to supply a name.

"Merkins."

"Merkins?" She shifted her shoulder as she considered. "Not DeValera?"

Joe DeValera was the chief of operations, so he was the more natural choice.

"No, Merkins has a better head on her shoulders."

"DeValera won't like that you're handing over responsibility to the CFO instead of to him. As COO, he'll expect to handle things while you get your feet under you."

"All the more reason he doesn't need more power. Write up a memo to all the executives explaining the decision. Make sure it sounds like DeValera's current responsibilities are too important and that no one else can do his job."

Sydney nodded, quickly taking a few notes for the memo she'd later write and send to Griffin for approval. As she did so, she couldn't help being impressed by his light hand when it came to managing the executive staff.

Something of her surprise must have shown in her expression because Griffin asked, "You disagree with my decision?"

She finished writing her notes as she shook her head. "No. On the contrary, I think it's a brilliant strategy." Griffin looked at her with his eyebrows raised, like he wanted her to say more, so she kept talking. "DeValera is very much your father's man. He's a good COO but a bit of a narcissist." As soon as the words were out of her mouth, she cringed. "I shouldn't have said that."

"I agree completely. And I don't trust him. With Hollister's health failing and this stupid quest of his—which, thankfully, no one outside the family knows about—the company was vulnerable enough before Dalton decided to step down. I don't want DeValera getting any ideas."

"That's very smart." She cringed a little, realizing she sounded like a yes-man.

"Then why do you look doubtful?"

She tilted her head, considering her next words. Just how honest did she want to be here? She never hesitated to give her opinion when Dalton asked for it, but he rarely asked.

"Out with it," Griffin ordered, his playful grin never slipping from his face.

"I just didn't expect you to have such insight into the inner workings of the company. That's all."

The smiled that twisted his lips suddenly looked just a little bitter. "Right."

"The strategy is brilliant," she hastened to reassure him.

"You just didn't think I was capable of it."

"It's not—" But she fumbled, unsure how to finish her sentence. And feeling just a smidge annoyed at him. "Look, you give off an air of…privileged indolence. I'm not the only one in the company who thinks this. Anyone would tell you the same thing." But suddenly she found she couldn't quite look him in the eye. Disconcerted by the idea that she didn't know him at all, she flipped the cover of her iPad closed, running her finger across the smooth blue leather. "But clearly you're not that guy. Obviously you haven't been ignoring the daily office politics of the company. Otherwise you wouldn't have noticed that Merkins has amassed a really great team or that DeValera is a power-hungry narcissist."

"Hey, narcissist is your word, not mine."

Her gaze snapped back to his and she saw that his smile hadn't changed at all. But perhaps his eyes were crinkling just a tad around the edges.

"All I'm saying—" her voice took on a defensive edge, but

she didn't try to hide it. It wasn't her fault he was that good at hiding his true nature "—is that you can't spend all that time and energy creating a persona to fool everyone and then be annoyed when you actually do fool everyone."

Griffin knew Sydney was right. He also knew her annoyance with him was totally justified. He'd kept a lot of things from her. There were sides of himself he shared with almost no one. Things he hadn't ever meant to share, even with her.

When he'd first started working for Cain Enterprises, he'd been pegged as the slacker in the family. At first, he hadn't courted that image on purpose. He simply hadn't wanted the job. But he had wanted the inheritance that would one day be his, and his father had made it clear that he'd never have one if he didn't accept the other. As it turned out, being a piss-poor executive left him plenty of time to work for Hope2O. Being known as the lazy one had made his life easier. Everyone he knew thought him either incapable or unwilling to work, so no one ever expected jack from him. No one within Cain Enterprises, anyway.

Generally speaking, he was okay with people thinking he was an ass and a playboy. So why was he annoyed that Sydney believed that, too?

Did he honestly think she somehow looked past the image he'd carefully cultivated to the man beneath? Would he want her to if she could?

It was hardly a fair question.

And Sydney was still standing before him, waiting for his response. And also looking rather nervous. She kept rubbing the pad of her thumb across the edge of her iPad cover as she frowned down at it as if she couldn't quite figure out where it had come from.

Finally, she straightened her shoulders and said, "If that's all?"

He pushed himself to his feet and sighed. "You're right.

And I'm not annoyed." Maybe if he said it often enough, he'd believe it. "I have no reason to be. If I act like a jerk, I have no one to blame but myself if that's how people see me."

Her expression was guarded, so he couldn't tell whether or not he'd placated her when she said, "Fine. I'll make that appointment for you with Merkins and have a draft of the letter to the officers."

"And let's see if we can get the board up here for a meeting by this evening. They've all seen that email from Dalton this morning. I don't want to give them too much time to think about things."

She had her iPad out again, making notes. After a second, she glanced up. "You might not realize this, but Dalton usually gives at least one week's notice because several of the board members—"

"Are out of town? Yes, I know. We'll video conference them in. Before we do anything else, we need to get me confirmed as interim CEO. Promise them it'll be a short meeting. I don't want to give them time to debate the alternatives."

"Very good."

"Also, I'll need to meet with Marion this afternoon and let her know I've changed positions."

"Will she expect to move up with you?"

"Probably not. She's used to coasting by without doing too much work. Besides, we'll need her to hold down the fort in the office of the VP of International Marketing until we can find someone else to fill that job."

She nodded, then closed the iPad again.

"Sydney—" he coaxed before she could vanish for good.

But she ignored the tone he'd used.

"Shall I schedule the meeting with Merkins for first thing in the morning? Say, eight o'clock?"

He did a quick mental review of his personal schedule. "Make it nine-thirty."

"Nine-thirty?" Sydney asked, frowning. "By then, everyone

will have been at work for several hours. Gossip will already be spreading. You need to get her on your side straightaway."

She was right, of course. Except he had a virtual meeting with a bank in Nairobi set up for eight in the morning. It had taken him two weeks to get the financial officer of the bank to even agree to the meeting. Rescheduling it would be a nightmare.

"I have another obligation at eight," he said, hoping she wouldn't argue with the note of finality in his voice.

He should have known better. Sydney set her jaw at a stubborn angle and flipped open her iPad again. "You don't. I took the liberty of having your assistant, Marion, forward your schedule to me earlier. Your morning is free."

"Marion doesn't have my complete schedule. I have a phone call to make at eight."

Sydney blew out a breath as though she was trying to muster her restraint. "Can you push it back?"

"No." It would be four in that part of Africa as it was. This was the best he'd been able to do.

Sydney pinched her mouth shut but then seemed unable to contain her ire. "You really don't want to blow this. DeValera will be looking for a way to shut you down. If he gets too much time with Merkins first—"

"Okay, eight-thirty. I'll try to move my other meeting forward." And he'd talk really fast.

She must have realized she'd gotten as much as she was going to because she gave a tight little nod. Then she added, "If you want to send me your personal schedule also, then I can put everything on a master schedule. Might make things easier for you."

"No. Marion never had access to my personal schedule. You don't need it, either."

"How can I function as your assistant if I don't know when or where you'll be?" she asked, frowning.

"Just run everything by me before you firm things up. That's how I did it with Marion."

Her frown deepened and her jaw clenched even tighter. "But I can't—"

"Marion made it work. So will you. It's just how I like to do things."

"Fine." But he could tell from the narrowing of her eyes that it wasn't fine at all. She spun on her foot to leave and he was pretty sure he heard her mutter, "If your personal life has to be that mysterious…"

He nearly called her back and explained the truth about his work for Hope2O but instead he kept his mouth shut.

Marion had been hired for him by his father's assistant. He'd liked Marion without ever really trusting her. And to be honest, as wily and cunning as Hollister was, Griffin wouldn't be surprised if the whole CEO office suite wasn't bugged.

Still he didn't want Sydney to think he was purposefully shutting her out—even if that was what he was doing.

"Wait a second." Instead of letting her leave, he stood and crossed to where she hovered near the door. He held out the folder he'd gotten from Dalton. "Here are all the notes from Dalton about his search for the heiress. Make copies for yourself and take an hour or so to look it over, then we'll talk more."

She looked from him to the folder and then back, finally meeting his gaze as she took the folder. Her expression was cautious but less openly distrustful than it had been just moments ago. "Okay."

"Look, I know I'm difficult to work with. And I know the company's in trouble. I'm going to do my damnedest not to screw it up any more than it already is. Let's just get through this. Together. Okay?"

"Okay." She tucked the folder on top of her iPad and left the office.

Alone in the room, Griffin was all too aware of the overbearing décor, the heavy French furniture and massive mahogany desk that had been in the office since Griffin's own childhood. The very walls seemed to close in on him.

Juggling the disparate elements of his life was typically something he excelled at. He kept his work for Cain separate from his work with Hope2O and his love life separate from both. He functioned best with everything compartmentalized.

He hadn't been lying to Sydney when he'd told her was going to try his damnedest not to screw anything up. That was true for the company and for his relationship with her.

Sydney worked furiously for the next couple of hours setting up the board meeting. The fact that every single member of the board was willing to rearrange his or her own schedule to be there—either in person or virtually—was either a good sign or a very bad one.

A half hour before the meeting she went across to the big conference room on the other side of the building to verify the folks in the IT department had gotten everything working for the board members who couldn't be physically present. She double-checked that catering had done their job, and she even removed one limp lily from the floral arrangement on the sideboard. Now everything was perfect.

This meeting had to go well. If the board didn't approve Griffin as interim CEO, she'd probably be out of a job. Yes, she'd find another one, but this was a good job, especially for someone as young as she was. She'd lucked into it. She'd first been hired as a temp when Dalton's previous assistant had knee surgery, but he'd kept her on when Janine had decided not to come back.

If she lost this job, her next position wouldn't pay nearly this well. Which meant making her mortgage payment would be a strain. It was already steep, but when she'd first bought her house, it had seemed like such a good investment. It had represented all the security she'd desperately wanted. Now, it just represented all that she'd lose if this didn't go well.

She left the conference room and hurried down the hall to her office. Griffin was leaving his as she walked in.

"I was just checking on the conference room. Everything looks good there."

"Thanks." He smiled that same breezy smile she was used to, the flash of white teeth and deep dimples. Suddenly the nerves she felt for the meeting morphed into a pleasant fluttery sort of anticipation that had nothing to do with efficient IT and catering departments.

She handed him the folio folder from her desk. "Here's your copy of the agenda. I kept it simple."

He flipped it open and read over it as she spoke. "Looks good."

He was about to walk out when she stopped him. "Wait a second. Is that what you're wearing?"

"Yeah." He glanced down as if seeing his jeans and shirt for the first time.

"You don't look the part of the business executive."

"I haven't exactly had time to go home and change."

She held up a hand to ward off a protest. "Just give me two minutes." She dashed into Dalton's office and dug around in the coat closet for a minute before returning. She held out what she'd found. "Here, put this on."

Griffin held it out in front of him. "A sweater?"

"Come on, trust me."

"A sweater?" he repeated, even as he pulled it over his head.

"I didn't have a lot to work with here." She helped him with the hem, tugging it over his hips. "Dalton keeps a couple of jackets here, but your shoulders are broader than his, so you couldn't wear one of those." Griffin stilled as she fussed over him, adjusting the sleeves of the V-neck sweater so a half-inch of cuff showed. Then she grabbed the two ties she'd found and held them up. "What do you think? Yellow or green?"

His lips twitched, dazzling her with a hint of white teeth and dimple. "How about no tie?"

"A tie says powerful and important," she argued.

"A tie with a sweater says Mr. Rogers," he countered, still smiling.

She rolled her eyes. "Trust me, nothing about you says Mr. Rogers."

Still, she conceded the point and set the ties aside, but she couldn't stop herself from reaching up to straighten his collar. Her fingers lingered on the warm skin of his neck and the faint bristle of growth along his jaw. He hadn't shaved this morning, she knew, but he must have shaved the night before. She thought about what the past twenty-four hours had been like for him. He'd called her as he'd left the airport—that had been around midnight. He must have shaved as soon as he'd gotten home, just before she showed up. She'd never thought about that until now...the way he always shaved just before they saw each other. The way his jaw was always smooth when he kissed her on her neck. And anywhere else.

Suddenly she realized they'd both gone completely still. Her breath caught in her chest as she looked up into his eyes, which were the exact same shade of blue as his shirt. Heat swirled through her body, turning her insides to mush and her knees to jelly.

Was he thinking about it, too? About the way he'd nuzzled her breast just last night? About the way he'd spread her body out before him like a feast and kissed every inch of her? How she'd done the same to him?

Abruptly, she dropped her hands and stepped away from him.

And this was why it wasn't a good idea to sleep with her boss. Up until now, she'd been so worried about the financial implications, she hadn't considered the emotional ones. How sex colored every interaction. How it could distract her. How it could mess with her priorities.

She grabbed a folder off the desk and thrust it toward him. "Here's the agenda."

He waggled the folder already in his hand. "You already handed me one."

"Oh." She glanced down. "This is a spare. In case you need it."

She looked up to see him watching her, the smile on his face broad, his eyes twinkling with amusement. As if he knew just how much he distracted her. "I think I'm good."

Oh, yeah. He was good. So damn good it damn nearly killed her.

"Okay then," she said, her tone overly bright. "Go hit it out of the park. Or whatever sports analogy fits."

"Don't worry. I've got this."

As he headed off to face the board, she had no doubt. He did have it.

He would win them over. He would convince them that he was fully qualified to be the CEO, just like he'd convinced her in the past few hours. He clearly understood how the company operated and what it needed. He even grasped the finer details of the personalities involved. He got people in a way that even Dalton had not. In that regard, he might even be a better CEO than Dalton had been.

But that didn't change any of her plans. She still needed to find the heiress because she needed to get Dalton back. If the past few minutes had shown her anything, it was that she couldn't do her job effectively if she was working for Griffin, not just because he distracted her and muddled her senses, but also because he made her doubt her own judgment. And because he was dangerous to her in a way no other man ever had been.

Five

"What do you think?" Griffin asked as he strolled into the conference room.

Three days had passed since the board had named Griffin interim CEO. As she had predicted, he'd won them over with little difficulty. They were not having the same luck with the search for Griffin's missing sister.

Sydney had laid out all her research on the conference table. In addition to the notes that Dalton had passed on to Griffin, she had stacks of her own notes and forty-two cardboard boxes Griffin's mother had had sent over. She hadn't even touched those yet. Frankly, she was hoping something like an actual lead would come along and she'd be saved the trouble.

Now, she glared up at him. "Seriously? Why are you out here again? You've checked on me every thirty minutes."

A mischievous smile spread across his lips. "This is how I work."

"Oh, really? When you were in your office down the hall, you'd come out every five minutes to distract Marion?"

His grin broadened. "Well, I do love Marion—and she does make a fantastic chocolate bread pudding for me every year on my birthday. But still—" he gave a hey-what-can-you-do kind of shrug "—come on."

"Right." She sighed. He didn't even have to finish the sentence. But she said it aloud anyway. "You've never slept with Marion."

"Of course I've never slept with Marion. I've known her since I was ten. She's like a mother to me."

Sydney scowled at him, even though it was herself she was irritated with. This was not the time to be flirting.

He must have taken her scowl to heart because he said, "Just to be clear, in addition to not sleeping together anymore, are we not supposed to talk about the fact that we slept together? Are we pretending it never even happened?"

She nearly snorted. If only it were that easy. How could she order him to pretend it hadn't happened if she couldn't do it herself?

"Let's just try not to talk about it, okay? My point is," she said sternly, or rather shooting for stern but landing somewhere vaguely in the area of disconcerted, "that even though you have every woman in this building wrapped firmly around your little finger, you'll find I am not so easy to—"

She broke off before she could get the rest of the sentence out of her mouth because she could practically see the innuendo forming on the tip of his tongue.

She waved aside his comment. "Yes, yes. I heard it. Can we just skip over all the jokes relating to the word *easy?*"

His grin broadened to the point he looked like the damn Cheshire cat.

"Look," she continued. "I'm trying to do the right thing here. Stop making this so difficult."

"But I'd hate to be the one accused of being easy." Before she could protest, he held up his hands in surrender. "Okay, okay. I'll let it go. I promise."

Although a smile still teased his lips, there was nothing malicious in his gaze. He wasn't teasing her to be mean; he just enjoyed the game too much to stop.

It was one of those unexpected things about him that she found so hard to resist. And this constant exposure to his charm made her feel…nervous. Off balance. Pursued in a way she never had experienced when they were merely sleeping together. Why was it so much easier to be around him when all his energy was focused on making her climax rather than on making her smile?

"Look," she said, "just stay on your side of the conference table and this will all go a lot more smoothly."

He frowned. "So it's not going well?"

She flipped closed the file in front of her. "You know this is insane, right?"

Griffin nodded with mock solemnity. "I do."

"Your father spent his entire life building this company and now he's threatening to throw it all away based on some anonymous letter he got."

"Exactly."

"And he's pitting you and your brothers against one another to try to find this girl."

"He is."

"Has it occurred to any of you that this girl might not even be real? I mean, obviously, whoever wrote the letter did it just to drive Mr. Cain crazy. She—or he—obviously—"

Griffin interrupted her. "He? The letter was written by a woman."

He reached over her to flip the folder back open and tapped his finger on the first page—a photocopy of the letter.

She picked it up and waved it around. "No, the letter was written by someone claiming to be a woman. Someone claiming to have had an affair with Hollister and claiming to have bore him a daughter. But there's no proof. No real evidence." She put the letter back on the top of the folder and considered it. "Which brings me back to my point. Whoever wrote the letter knew him well enough to want revenge and to know this would drive him crazy. But that doesn't mean that the person who wrote the letter was actually the girl's mother. Or that there even is a girl."

"Hmm." Griffin stood, stroking his chin as he paced the length of her office and back, considering her words. "Good point. But it's irrelevant."

"How so?"

"It doesn't matter who wrote the letter or even whether or not there's a girl to find. Proving there isn't a girl would be harder than finding one. It's like proving there isn't life on another planet. It'd be damn near impossible."

"Well, it might be damn near impossible to find her even if she does exist."

Griffin gave her a level look. "So you think Laney's theory was wrong? You don't think this nanny, Vivian, is the one?"

Sydney flipped back through the file to find the color copy she'd made of the photos Laney had found. The first picture was of two women and a girl standing on the beach somewhere. As Sydney understood it, the older woman was Matilda Fortino, Laney's grandmother. She'd been the Cain's housekeeper for Dalton and Griffin's entire childhood. Dalton had gone to see her because he'd thought that if anyone had the dirt on his father, it would be her. His search had brought him to Laney, whom he'd apparently been in love with when he was younger. As hard a time as Sydney had imagining Dalton—her serious and stoic boss—falling in love at all, she was glad that he seemed to have found happiness, even if he hadn't found his missing sister.

But Laney had believed the girl in this photo might be the missing girl. There was another picture of the girl's mother stapled behind the first. In that picture, she was still pregnant and she had her arm around the shoulder of another pregnant woman—Laney's mother. More importantly, the picture had been taken in the Cain's backyard.

Laney's grandmother had Alzheimer's and could tell them nothing about the young woman or the girl. However—according to Laney's notes—Matilda's incoherent ramblings had led Laney to believe that the woman had a connection to Hollister, a connection that might have put her in danger.

Was all this conjecture, or was this a real lead?

Sydney looked at the two pictures and frowned. "I don't know," she said finally. "The connection seems specious at best."

"I know. It isn't a lot to go on."

Sydney looked up to study Griffin, but once again she was frustrated by his chameleon charm. His mouth was twisted into a smile, but she couldn't read his emotions. Was he as doubtful as she was, or did he believe this girl on the beach was his sister?

Glancing down at the picture, he said, "It would help if whoever took the picture was close enough to see the girl's eyes."

"Why?"

"Well, if she had Cain-blue eyes, then we'd know for sure Hollister was her father."

"Cain-blue?" Sydney asked.

"Sure. Didn't you ever notice that my eyes and Dalton's are the same color?"

"No" She couldn't keep her skepticism from her voice. "Blue eyes are blue eyes. But you and Dalton look nothing alike."

"Maybe not," Griffin chided. "But our eyes are almost identical."

Before she could scoff, he grabbed her hand and tugged her gently to her feet, positioning her to stand between his outstretched legs.

"Look," he gently urged her. "Tell me Dalton and I don't have the same eyes."

She had no choice but to gaze into Griffin's eyes. Standing this close, she was hit with the scent of him. All fresh and minty. His hand, warm and dry, still clenched one of hers. His thumb rubbed idly across the back of her hand. She was struck by how gentle his touch, but how rough his skin, was.

She had been touched by him enough—and intimately at that—that she knew the skin on his hands was roughened as if by hard manual labor, but for the life of her, she'd still couldn't imagine what he might be doing in his spare time to earn those calluses.

Giving her head a little shake, she tried to focus on his eyes.

"Well, for starters, the shape of your eyes is totally different. His eyes are rounder. Yours are more almond shaped. And crinkly."

"You're saying I squint?" he teased, his hands releasing hers to settle on her hips. With nowhere else to put them, she dropped her own hands to his waist.

"No," she harumphed. "I'm saying you laugh. Dalton never laughs. Besides, Dalton has this way of looking right through someone. His eyes have this soulless quality. It's not disdain or annoyance. Just disinterest."

Griffin chuckled. "Exactly. So what about me?"

And this was what stumped her.

"You…really look at people," she began slowly. Sometimes, when he looked at her, she felt as though he could see into her very soul, but she wasn't going to say that aloud. "And I'm not entirely sure that's a good thing because sometimes I'm still not sure if you smile because you enjoy being with people or if human nature amuses you."

The smile slowly faded from his expression and she felt the tension in his hands. Like he was trying to decide if he should push her away or pull her closer.

Part of her knew she should probably stop talking right then and there, but instead she finished her thought.

"But you're not a cruel man, so I don't think it's that you're laughing at people. It's more like…just another way of keeping people at a distance."

She kept her gaze pinned to the top button of his shirt while she spoke, all too aware that she was just guessing about him but that her guesses revealed as much about her as they did about him. If he was really paying attention. And maybe he wasn't.

He gently cupped her chin and tipped it up so she met his gaze. "Is that what you think? That I push people away?"

It's what I do.

But she didn't say that aloud. Instead, she asked, "Do you?"

"Doesn't everybody?"

"Yes, I suppose everybody does."

Suddenly this whole conversation felt way too intimate. Even more intimate than the time they'd spent in bed together because that had been about sex, not emotion. And if there was one thing she was good at, it was separating her physical needs from her emotional needs.

So—though she'd told herself that she wasn't going to sleep with him again now that he was her boss—she gave into every urge she'd been suppressing for the past twenty-four hours. She threaded her fingers up through his hair, luxuriating in the feel of the thick, long strands. She let herself lean into him. And she inhaled deeply, letting the warm spicy scent of him invade her senses.

His hands clenched on her hips and this time she had no doubt about his intention because he pulled her close to him, rocking his hips against the juncture of her legs. He dipped his head down to her neck and left a trail of kisses along the sensitive skin there.

His breath was hot against her skin as he murmured, "Isn't this crossing that line you drew in the sand?"

"Yes, damn it." She wished he hadn't brought it up, but she couldn't fault him for it, either. She was the one who'd set the boundary. She couldn't begrudge him for respecting her wishes, even if he was ignoring her desires.

She gave his waist a quick squeeze, relishing the way his muscles clenched in response to her touch, and then she stepped back.

She smoothed her hands down her sleek tan sweater and gave the hem a tug. "What were we even talking about?"

"Cain-blue eyes," Griffin said easily, apparently less befuddled than she was.

Right. The Cain eyes.

That was the discussion that had led her astray. And—she now realized—she'd never even really responded to the comment. She'd gone and rambled on and on about the shape of his eyes and the character of his smile, but she'd never really admitted that, yes, he and Dalton had eyes that were exactly the same piercing shade of blue. Not bright sky-blue or deep indigo-blue, but an eerie sort of sea-blue, turquoise almost, pale in the center with a dark ring of contrast.

She knew intimately the shade of Griffin's eyes—just as she knew their shape. But she was only vaguely aware of what Dalton's eyes looked like.

"Well," she said brusquely, "even if we could see her eyes, that would tell us nothing. The girl could have brown eyes and still be Hollister's daughter."

"Nah. If she's Hollister's daughter, she has blue eyes."

"You're just assuming the girl's mother didn't have a brown-eye gene to contribute to the pool?"

Griffin waggled his hand in a maybe/maybe not gesture.

"My instinct tells me that whoever she was, the girl's mother would have had blue eyes. My father definitely had a type. My mother, Cooper's mother and his other longtime mistress all looked like they could have been sisters."

It took a second for the full meaning of his words to sink in. When they did, she raised her eyebrows in question and asked, "Seriously?"

He gave a dismissive shrug. "Yeah. He liked waifish blondes. The more fragile-looking the better. And they were all blue-eyed."

She kept looking at him, waiting for him to pick up on her train of thought. When he didn't, she gave his shoulder a playful shove. "Not that, idiot. I mean, your father had a long-term mistress and no one thought to question her?"

"Sharlene doesn't know anything."

"Sharlene? Why does that name sound familiar?"

"How should I know?"

"Sharlene is a pretty unusual name. You're not talking about Sharlene Sheppard, are you?"

"She was Sharlene Davonivich then, but yeah. Why?"

"And this was before she married Jack Sheppard, your father's business rival?" she asked.

"Actually, this was before Jack Sheppard was his business rival. They used to be partners. Things went bad sometime after Sharlene and my father broke up."

Sydney let out a low whistle. "Sometimes the history of Cain Enterprises reads like an Italian opera."

Griffin looked slightly abashed. "Yeah. Heartache. Epic rivalries. It's like *Les Misérables* but without all the singing."

She chuckled, then asked, "Are you sure she's not involved? How long were they together?"

Griffin shrugged. "Ten years, maybe."

"Ten years? Forget what she knows. Forget this wild goose chase after a pregnant nanny who may or may not have even slept with Hollister. If this Sharlene person was your father's mistress for ten years, then she could be the girl's mother."

"No."

"But you said yourself that your father was selective about who he let get close to him."

"Sharlene doesn't have any children."

"Maybe she gave the baby up for adoption." She was really warming to the idea now. It just made sense. "And if she did, that would certainly explain the bitterness in the letter."

"No," Griffin said. "Sharlene was never pregnant."

"You can't know that for sure. Sometimes when women don't want people to know they're pregnant, they hide the pregnancy for as long as they can. They go away for the last few months, give birth in private. They—"

"Sharlene wasn't the type. She and my father never hid their affair."

"As far as you know."

Griffin's hands rested low on her waist and he rubbed his thumb across her hip bone absently as he spoke. "You're right. I'm not a hundred percent certain. But Sharlene was like another mother to me."

He seemed completely unaware of what his hands were doing, but it drove her crazy.

She tried to step away, but his grip on her was surprisingly strong. "So it's only natural you don't want to consider that she might have been the one to write the letter."

"Actually, what I was going to say is that when I was a kid, I saw her at least once a week, sometimes more often. If she'd been pregnant, I would remember it. If she'd gone away, even for a few months, I would have noticed."

Sydney frowned, realizing he was right. He probably would have remembered it.

"Besides," he continued, finally letting her go. "When they broke up, it was nasty. If she'd had the kind of leverage a kid would have given her, she'd have used it then."

"You don't know—"

"I do know." His tone was harsher than she'd ever heard it before; all traces of the easygoing charmer she knew so well were gone.

For a moment, all she could do was stare at him blankly. Then she nodded. "Okay. So Sharlene isn't the girl's mother. But we should still talk to her. She might know something."

He stared at her for a long moment before finally nodding. "Okay. I'll give her a call. See if she knows anything."

Before she could say anything else, Griffin disappeared back into his office and she was left standing beside the conference table, wondering exactly what she'd said that had driven a wedge between them. And what she'd gotten herself into.

If she was honest with herself, it wasn't the family drama that surprised her; it was Griffin's reaction to it. She'd been with him for four months, for goodness sake. They'd had sex countless times. Spent entire weekends in bed eating takeout and watching cheesy monster movies on Syfy.

So how was it there were so many things she didn't know about him?

Before she could ponder that question anymore, her phone buzzed. She glanced down to see a text from Jen.

As she typed in a quick response, she shrugged off the question altogether. There were plenty of things he didn't know about her, either. Things she would never tell him. That wasn't the kind of relationship they had.

Suddenly, that made her sad, even though she wasn't quite sure why.

It felt as though their relationship had shifted inexplicably in the past few days. Yeah, sure, there was that huge obvious shift. He was her boss now. They weren't sleeping together anymore. Yeah, all *that* stuff had happened. But there was something else going on, too. She was seeing a side of Griffin that she'd never seen before. Something beyond that surface charm she'd originally been attracted to.

The problem was, now that she knew there was more to him than that, could they ever go back to the relationship they'd had before? She didn't think so. Now that she'd seen this Griffin, this guy who cared about the company and who worked as hard as he played, she'd never be able to forget he existed. Even if Dalton did come back and she was no longer working for Griffin. She'd never be able to go back to just sleeping with him, either. So where did that leave her?

Even before Griffin had taken over as CEO, she'd worried she was in over her head. She blamed that damned key. Why had everything become so complicated? Working with him every day constantly strained her willpower. She didn't know how much longer she'd be able to keep him at arm's length.

She could only hope they found this girl soon. Once Dalton reclaimed his position as CEO, she'd have a little distance from Griffin. Going cold turkey would be so much easier without having him tempt her constantly. But what if Dalton never came back? It was a possibility she couldn't let herself consider. They would find the girl. Dalton would come back. Griffin wouldn't be her boss forever.

She just had to make damn sure they found her soon.

Six

"How's it going?" Griffin asked from the doorway to the conference room.

Sydney looked from the stack of papers in front of her to Griffin and back with her eyebrows raised. "How does it look like it's going?"

That signature smile of his crept across his face. "Slowly. It looks like it's going slowly."

She gave an indelicate snort. "Exactly. Your powers of observation are astonishing."

It had been two days since the conversation about Sharlene. That conversation that she'd been so sure had changed everything. And yet...nothing had changed. By the time she'd left work that day, Griffin had returned to his normal self. The next morning, she'd briefly considered asking him whether he'd actually called Sharlene, as she'd suggested. Instead, she gritted her teeth and started going through the Cain household records. Forty-two boxes in all. Sydney had dug into the boxes and started looking for any references to a nanny named Vivian.

Part of her said she was being a coward. The other part pointed out calmly that she was just doing her job. This was what Griffin had asked her to do, so she was doing it. If he wanted her doing anything else, he'd tell her.

The part that thought she was being a coward noted that Griffin was stubbornly ignoring the obvious. That he needed to go talk to Sharlene—and possibly his mother also—because a real conversation with an actual human would get him further than countless hours searching through boxes would.

The problem was, as much as she wanted to pretend otherwise, Griffin wasn't just her boss. He'd been her lover first. She knew his personal needs and his professional ones. If this was Dalton she was dealing with, there'd be no question. She would just trust her gut. But with Griffin, she had no idea if her gut was telling her to do what was right for the company or what was right for her man. Or maybe it wasn't her gut doing the talking at all. Maybe this was unfulfilled sexual tension speaking. Because once she found the heiress, maybe she could justify getting back in Griffin's bed.

She looked at him, trying not to appreciate his broad shoulders or the little bit of stubble scattered across his jaw. Since taking over as CEO, he'd traded in his rugged jeans for twill slacks and his linen shirts for crisp, pressed cotton. Somehow the fact that he still left the shirts untucked until right before he went into meetings made the look that much more appealing. The result was that he always came across as just a little rumpled and disreputable. It lent an air of intimacy to the office. And, frankly, it made her want to rip his clothes off.

To keep her hands occupied—and off his buttons—she flipped the lid off box number nineteen. "I've been at this for days now. I'm not even halfway through these records. And so far, all I can tell you is that your mother spends too much on shoes and your parents' accountant pays the bills on time."

"I could have told you that," he said with a smile.

"We're never going to make any progress here."

"You think the information is buried too deep?" he asked.

She picked up a sheaf of papers. Printouts from the early eighties. Old reams of accordion-style paper. The ink from the dot-matrix printer was faded and damn near impossible to read. In addition, the pages were so damn musty, she was pretty sure an entire colony of dust mites was vacationing in her sinuses. She lifted the bottom edge of the stack with her thumb and let it fan through the hundred or so pages.

"I've been through every page of your parents' household records. From the year Laney was born and for two years in either direction, just to be sure. There is no mention of anyone named Vivian. Not anywhere in these records."

Griffin was watching her in that way he had, quietly attentive. The way that made her think he caught all the subtleties going on beneath the surface. That he knew that her eyes ached from staring at the blurred ink. That her back twitched from sitting too long. And, most especially, that every time she'd gotten sleepy from just sitting there going through the pages, she'd given herself a two-minute break to fantasize about locking his office door and doing crazy things to his body. And about the way he liked to drive her completely crazy with lust before taking her. And the powerful way he drove into her. And the way he hooked her ankles up over his arms so her hips were at just the right angle.

And she knew, instantly, that she should not have let that image flit through her brain because she could feel her cheeks heating up. And damn it, now he would definitely know what she'd been thinking, even if he was only guessing before.

Hoping to distract them both, she pushed her chair back and stood, walking over to the water cooler beside the credenza on the far side of the conference room and pouring herself a tiny cup of water.

But when she turned back around, it was to find him watching her. His gaze was hot and she could feel the weight of it against her skin as potent as a physical touch. Crap, she'd distracted him all right, but not in the way she'd meant to.

She swallowed most of the water in one gulp, nearly drowning herself.

"Is it too hot in here for you?" he asked, his voice pitched low with innuendo. "'Cause I could turn the air-conditioning back on for you."

"No, thanks. I know right where the air-conditioning controls are."

"Oh, I know you do." He grinned wickedly and she knew he was thinking of the time he'd all but begged her to pleasure herself while he watched. The resulting earth-shattering sex was no doubt seared into both of their minds. "I was just offering to take care of it for you. If you wanted me to."

Damn, but she did want him to take care of it for her. Right here. Right now.

But that was the very last thing she could do. Because the only thing worse than sleeping with your boss was sleeping with your boss in the middle of the day on the middle of the executive board table.

"Ugh, this is so frustrating. It feels like we're never going to get anywhere like this." Especially because the only place she wanted to get was into Griffin's pants. Yeah, *frustrating* was the perfect word. Unfortunately. "I wish we could just talk to your mother about it."

Griffin gave a bark of shocked laughter. "Why?"

She shrugged. Wasn't it obvious? "Presumably she could tell us exactly who this nanny is."

"I doubt that."

"You don't think she'd remember?"

He gave a snort. "I'd be shocked if she ever knew the woman's name to begin with."

"I find that hard to believe." What kind of woman wouldn't know the name of her children's nanny?

"Do you remember Mrs. Fortino?" he asked.

"Yes. She's Laney's grandmother. She was your housekeeper for years, right?"

"Exactly. Thirty years. I was fourteen when I realized my mother had been saying her name wrong. With an *A* on the end instead of an *O*."

"So? That's an easy mistake to make."

"Yeah, sure. So I corrected my mother. We fought over it. My mother refused to admit she was wrong. Finally, my mother called Mrs. Fortino in and told her that regardless of what her name actually was, from that moment on she was to go by Mrs. Fortina in my mother's presence. She told the poor women that if anyone addressed her by her real name, she would be instantly fired."

"That's absurd. You can't fire an employee over something like that," Sydney protested.

"When you're a self-indulgent narcissist you can do whatever you want if other people let you get away with it. Mrs. Fortino merely nodded and asked if that was all. As soon as she left, my mother told me to never again interfere with the way she ran the household."

"You think she did it to punish you?"

"She did it because she wanted me to know she was in charge."

His cold conviction unsettled her. She knew, of course, that he wasn't particularly close to his family, but she'd written it down as a peculiarity of the rich.

"Well, that's certainly not very nice, but it has nothing to do with this."

"I didn't tell you the story to elicit your sympathy. I told you to explain why I don't think talking to Mother would make any difference."

"Surely she's not that bad."

"I think they said the same thing about Nero's mother."

"Oh, come on." She sent him a teasing smile. "You're comparing her to one of the most reviled women in history? Did she commit murder? Are there plots to overthrow the government I don't know about?"

"Wow, you really know your Roman history."

"What can I say? I liked *I, Claudius.* My point is, a simple conversation with your mother might answer many of our questions."

"First off, there's no such thing as a simple conversation with my mother. And second, a conversation with her has never made any situation better."

Sydney stared down at the open file in front of her, gnawing on her lip as she considered her next words. Sure, just asking him was the most straightforward course of action, but she was definitely treading on new ground here. They didn't have the kind of relationship where they talked about their families or their childhoods. He'd already revealed more to her now than he ever had before. And if it was just human curiosity driving her, she would have let it go. But there was far more at stake here than her fascination with this man. If they didn't find the heiress, the future of the entire company was at stake. Thousands of people would be out of work, herself included.

"You really don't like your mother, do you?" she quipped, trying to make light of an obviously difficult situation.

"What gave me away?" He smiled at her. It was an expression very similar to his normal charming grin but without any warmth in his gaze. "Was it the comparison to Nero's murderous mother?"

She ignored his glib words and asked, "Why?"

He blinked in surprise. "What?"

"Why don't you like her? Or more to the point, why are you so angry at her about this?" She gestured to the mess of papers in front of her, partly to indicate the mass of files his mother had sent over, but also referencing the mess with his father. "This thing with the missing heiress? That's your father's mistake, not hers. She's the victim here—"

"My mother is never a victim," he interrupted.

"She's just as much a victim as you. Maybe more so. The way I understand it, in his original will she was going to receive ten percent. Now, no matter what happens, she gets nothing."

"You think I'm being too hard on her?" His voice was flat.

"I don't know. I guess I just…" She stared down at the page in front of her. One of the corners curled up, and she ran her fingers back and forth over it so it rolled and unrolled. "I get why you're angry at your father over this. I get that. But I don't understand why you seem to be mad at your mother, too."

Without really meeting her eyes, he rounded the board table that dominated the room and crossed to the antique bar that stood in one corner. In her months here, she'd never seen Dalton—or anyone else for that matter—pour themselves a drink in the middle of a meeting. However, Dalton kept the bar there because that was the kind of businessman his father had been. Apparently, among Texas oil men of that generation, a deal wasn't considered sealed until you'd shared a drink over it. It all seemed very *Dallas* to her.

Even though she'd never seen Griffin drink before now, he poured himself a Scotch and tossed it back quickly before pouring himself another.

Finally, he turned and faced her, the glass cradled in his hand, his legs stretched out in front of him as he leaned back against the bar. "You're right. My father is a lying, cheating bastard and he always has been." He took a drink before continuing. "But at least he never pretended to be anything other than what he was. He never hid the fact that he'd do anything to increase Cain Enterprises profits. He never lied about the other women. He's a bastard, but he's an honest bastard. My mother, however, spent our childhoods alternately pretending to be the perfect loving mother and ignoring us completely."

She studied him with a tilted head. "What makes you think she was pretending? Maybe she really was a loving mother."

"Let me ask you this. What would you have done in her shoes?"

His question surprised her so much, she blinked in surprise. "What do you mean?"

He pushed himself away from the bar and took a slow step toward her. "What would you do in her shoes? What would you do if your husband cheated on you?"

"I don't know. I've never thought about it." But everything inside her recoiled from the idea. She wouldn't tolerate it. Still, every woman was different. "I guess if I still loved him, I might try to make it work. Marriage counseling. Something like that."

"No," Griffin said, and at first she thought he was arguing with her logic. But he took another step toward her. "No. Pretend you don't love him at all. That you only married him for the money. Would you stay with him? Just for the money?"

"I would never marry someone just for the money."

"Pretend for a second that you would. Pretend that you were rich already and could have married anyone, but you chose someone so ambitious and ruthless, you knew he could make you rich beyond belief. And then pretend he turned out to be just as ruthless in his personal life. Pretend he slept with whoever he wanted and humiliated you in public and in front of your friends. Would you stay?"

"No." She felt the flame of embarrassment for his mother just listening to him. Not just embarrassment, but anger, too. At Griffin, for so ruthlessly displaying his mother's shortcomings. Anger made her meet his gaze as she defended his mother. "But everyone is different. I can't judge her for staying. I don't know her well enough."

"Well, pretend for a second that you would stay with a man you abhorred. Pretend you'd put up with his cheating and his mistresses. Pretend you'd put up with it for more than a decade because the money was just that important to you. Pretend you're just that stubborn or proud or greedy. Now pretend that the same man who stomps all over you every chance he gets treats your kids just as badly as he treats you."

She dropped her gaze as she felt the bottom drop out of her

stomach. She licked her lips because her mouth had suddenly gone dry. Suddenly she understood why he harbored so much anger toward his mother. Suddenly she got it.

"No." Her voice came out as a whisper. She didn't have kids. She didn't even know if she would ever have kids—at least, not biological kids. She'd always had the idea of doing the foster kid thing someday. If she did have kids—biological or foster—she would do everything in her power to protect them. "No, I wouldn't."

Griffin nodded, then tossed back the rest of his drink and set the glass down with a thud. "Yeah. That's what I thought."

With that, he turned and walked out.

He didn't have to say anything else. Because now she got it. His father may be a bastard, but that didn't really bother him because he'd never really cared about his father. He'd loved his mother. He probably still did. Despite everything, he would love her. That, more than anything, explained why he harbored so much anger and resentment. He loved her, but he was constantly disappointed by her.

She felt the same way about her own biological mother. She'd lived with her for the first six years of her life. Of course she'd loved her. And, of course, all kinds of negative emotions were mixed in with the love, but it was the love that made all of it hurt.

She understood that maybe better than anyone else.

But she was also an outsider in Griffin's relationship with his mother. She could see, perhaps more clearly than he could, just how complicated this was. Unfortunately, none of this insight into the Cain family solved anything. None of this got her any closer to finding the heiress.

One of Griffin's lifelong goals was to never be as much of an ass as his father. In fact, his goal was to never do anything like his father. Yet here he was, bullying his subordinate, bitching about his mother, Caro Cain, and drinking in the middle of the morning. In short, he was acting just like his dad. Funny how that had worked out.

Back in his office—Dalton's office, really—he plunked himself down in Dalton's chair, scrubbed a hand down his face, swallowed back his regrets and tried to think of how to dig his way out of this mess. First step, naturally, was to find something to eat. It was only ten, but breakfast had been a bowl of oatmeal five hours ago. He could feel the Scotch eating its way through the oats right now.

One of the peppermints Dalton always kept in his desk would do for starters. He unwrapped one of the Brach's candies and plopped it in his mouth. Then he started pulling open drawers looking for some nuts or a granola bar or something. He knew Dalton well enough to figure that the guy had probably eaten about half his meals right here at this desk.

Tucked into the back of the second drawer, he found something far more interesting than a pack of almonds. Behind the stack of files was a nine-by-eleven manila envelope with the word *Confidential* stamped on the front. The return address was from a company out of L.A. that Dalton sometimes used to do employee background checks. Not the normal HR kind, either. The hardcore kind. Panic spiked through Griffin. This company did the kind of background check that would reveal a VP's involvement with an international charity. Did Dalton know about Hope2O? If he did, then why the hell had he left Griffin in charge of Cain Enterprises?

In the bottom drawer, he found a jar of almonds and he poured a few out into his hand before opening the manila folder and pulling out the pages it contained. It took him several minutes of staring at the file before he realized what it contained—that was how surprised he was by the envelope's contents.

It wasn't a file on him. It was information about Sydney.

Dalton must have subcontracted the work when he'd decided to hire her full-time. Yeah, HR would handle all the reference checks and job recommendations, but it wasn't uncommon for Dalton to hire out a more in-depth background search for someone in a position of authority at the company. And now that Griffin thought about it, that certainly described Sydney's position. She knew everything about the company and had access to some very high-level stuff. She had more influence than most of the junior VPs. Certainly more than he had. So it only made sense. Still, he hadn't been expecting it, so seeing the file surprised the hell out of him.

He mindlessly popped a few almonds into his mouth as he flipped through the pages. He hadn't meant to read it. If he hadn't been hungry and tired and just drunk two shots of Scotch in quick succession, he would have had the foresight to shove the pages back into the envelope and let it go.

Instead, his gaze scanned the pages almost without realizing he was doing it. And once he'd read some of it, he couldn't stop. In fact, he had to read parts a second time, just because it all seemed so damn hard to believe. So completely out of character with the woman he knew.

Finally, he shoved the pages back into the envelope and buried it at the back of the drawer. He ate more nuts, hoping the salt would quell the queasy feeling in his stomach. It didn't.

If he hadn't felt like a total jackass before, he certainly did now. Here he'd been bitching about his sad childhood as the poor, ignored rich boy, and Sydney had real tragedy in her background. She was one bowl of porridge short of being a character in a Dickens novel. And he'd had the gall to complain to her.

He was surprised she hadn't thrown his drink in his face and walked out on him right then.

Naturally, his first impulse was to apologize. But to do so he'd have to admit what he'd done, which would relieve his own guilt, but she wouldn't be happy about it. Somehow, he didn't think this was the kind of information she'd share with just everyone. After all, they'd been sleeping together for months and she hadn't mentioned that she'd been a foster child.

That Child Protective Services had removed her from her birth mother when she was six. Of course, before this morning, he hadn't trotted out his pathetic tortured past, either. He hated being the object of pity and he suspected that Sydney felt the same way. No. It would be much better if he didn't tell her at all. If he just buried the information in the nether regions of his brain and forgot all about it.

Which still left him with the issue of how to make it up to her for acting like an ass earlier. But that was an issue easily resolved.

He pushed back his chair and dropped the now empty almond container in the trash. On his way out of the office, he stopped back by the conference room. Sydney looked up as he stuck his head in the door, her expression wary.

Before she could ask, he said, "I'm going to follow your advice and go talk to my mother. See what she knows."

Surprise flickered over Sydney's face. "You are?"

"Yeah. I figure maybe you're right about her. Maybe she can help."

"Do you think she will?" Sydney closed the file in front of her and leaned forward eagerly. "I mean, she has nothing at stake in this. If she's anything like you've described, maybe she won't want to help."

Strangely, that idea hadn't actually occurred to him. "She might not be able to help. Her help might be more of a hindrance—" He gestured to the boxes to make his point. "But I'm sure she'll want to help."

"Even if finding the heiress gets her nothing?"

"She won't see it that way. If I find the heiress, she knows I won't cut her off cold. Dalton would never have done that, either, though I'm not sure if she'd have thought it through. It's Cooper she has to worry about. Well, that and the whole shebang reverting to the state. No, she and I may not have a great relationship, but she knows I'll treat her fairly. She'll help if she can." Sydney smiled so brightly, he added, "I'm still not sure how helpful she'll be, but I'll try."

Sydney's grin didn't diminish a bit. "Thank you!"

In that moment she looked so lovely that he wanted to cross the room, pull her into his arms and kiss her. Not the kind of soul-searing kiss that would lead to her spread over the conference table naked, but a simple kiss. The kind that would honor the delicacy of her beauty. The kind that would salve the wounds of a broken childhood. The kind that would promise her a lifetime of safety, security and emotional support.

But he didn't know how to make those kinds of promises, let alone how to keep them, so instead he just nodded and walked away.

Seven

Traffic in Houston sucked. It always did. But for once, Griffin didn't curse the snarl of cars slowing his trip to his parents' house. He did not relish the upcoming conversation or the maternal theatrics that were sure to accompany it. The traffic on the loop was practically at a standstill, so instead of getting on, he pulled into a nearby parking lot and used the Bluetooth in his car to put in a call to Carl Nichols, his second in command at Hope2O.

He hadn't yet told Carl about what was going on with Cain Enterprises. Until now, some part of him had genuinely believed that this would all blow over. That after a couple of days of crazy sex with Laney, Dalton would come to his senses and ask for his job back. But apparently, a little sanity on his brother's part was too much to ask for. And because finding the heiress was proving more difficult than he'd expected, Griffin figured it was time to come clean with Carl so that things at Hope2O wouldn't devolve too much while his own attention was elsewhere.

After Griffin explained, Carl was silent for a long minute. Then he said, "That sounds more like something you would do."

Griffin snorted. "Right. I'll just walk away from a half billion dollars."

"Why not? Dalton did."

"Dalton also got offers from ten other Fortune 500 companies within about five minutes of quitting."

"Do you want to work for another Fortune 500 company?"

"Don't be an ass," Griffin said lightly. "You know I don't want a job somewhere else. I barely do the job I have, even though it's practically part-time. The only reason I've stayed at Cain Enterprises for as long as I have is because I want to get my hands on my inheritance so I can put it to work at Hope2O."

"Right. And now your practically part-time job has turned into a full-time position as CEO."

"Interim CEO," Griffin interrupted.

"Interim or not, you're going to have a hell of a time keeping up with that job and this one."

Griffin glared at the sea of red brake lights still clogging the loop. "You're right. But I don't see any way around it. Either I do this job or I forfeit a fortune."

Carl was silent for a long moment, then spoke with disappointment in his voice. "And you just can't give up the money."

"You know the money doesn't mean jack to me. Hope2O needs the money. Not me."

"No, Hope2O needs you on board all the time. It's your expertise we need, not your money."

"You think I should walk away like Dalton did?"

"Hey, I can't tell you what to do. I've never had a carrot worth half a billion dollars, but ask yourself this—what has the promise of all that money ever gotten you?"

Griffin didn't have an answer to that. The conversation moved on to other Hope2O business, and he stayed on the phone with Carl taking care of obligations he'd been neglecting for a week until long after the traffic on the loop cleared up. It was well after noon when he finally got back on the road and finished the drive to his parents'. All the while, in the back of his mind was the question Carl had posed. What had all the Cain money ever gotten him?

Because Griffin was going to talk to his mother, Sydney felt no compunction abandoning her drudgery to head back to her desk so she could catch up on her normal duties as EA to the CEO. After a morning away from her work, things had started to pile up. The whole EA thing hadn't exactly been the career path she'd imagined for herself when she'd done her undergraduate work in psychology. She'd always imagined she'd do postgraduate study and one day get her therapist's license. She'd taken her first job as an assistant on a whim. Just something to pay the bills while she'd waited for the next semester to start. But she was good at it. The money was great, and she found being in the thick of things in an office surprisingly rewarding. Today was no different. Fifty fires had sprouted up during her morning away from the computer, and she doused them with her usual speed and efficiency. Her inner therapist laughed at her. The joy she took in her job was an obvious attempt to fill her need to be needed. To feel like none of it could function without her. She knew that's why she loved it and she didn't even mind.

She was cruising through her work when the phone rang. "Griffin Cain's office. How can I help you?"

"Is Griffin available?" asked a woman's cool voice.

"He's not in right now. I may be able to transfer you to his cell phone. May I ask who's calling?"

There was an annoyed huff as though the caller had expected Sydney to recognize her voice. "This is Caro Cain. I am allowed to call my own son, aren't I?"

"I'm sorry, Mrs. Cain. I'll patch you through." But the phone rang and rang and Griffin never picked up. Sydney switched back over to the original call and apologized again. "I'm sorry, Mrs. Cain. I'd be happy to connect you to his voice mail or take a message. Was this in regard to the conversation you had this morning?"

There was a pause and then, with a touch of uncertainty in her voice, Caro asked, "The conversation?"

"Yes. The conversation," Sydney repeated, feeling dumb. "Griffin left the office, oh…nearly three hours ago." Surely that was enough time to get to his parents' house. If he hadn't gone there, then where had he gone? "He said he was going to your house to talk to you." Unless Caro wasn't at home. That explained it. "Are you at home? Perhaps he missed you?"

"You may be my son's assistant, but I hardly think I need to clear my schedule with you." There was a pinched quality to Caro's voice. "What did he want to discuss with me?"

Sydney hesitated, her mind flooding with all the negative things Griffin had said about his mother. But he was the one who'd said he planned to go talk to her. Surely no harm could come from her just giving Caro a glimpse of his cards.

"He wanted to talk to you about the missing heiress. We've hit a little roadblock in the course of our research and he thought you would be able to help him narrow down the search."

"He did?" Caro sounded surprised, but she recovered quickly. "Well, of course he did. I was at the house all morning. I wonder why he didn't come."

Sydney nearly harumphed. Caro wasn't the only one with questions. It wasn't that Griffin had to tell her where he was going to be every second of every day, but his disappearing act was getting old. As his assistant, it was her job to know his whereabouts, and frankly she was getting tired of feeling left in the dark.

"I wish he had just called. I've already left the house and won't be back until this evening." Apparently, Caro felt the same way as Sydney. The other woman sighed and then continued in a confidential tone. "We could have talked this morning and been done with it. As it is, it could be sometime tomorrow before he catches up with me. Valuable time is wasting and he's off doing God only knows what."

Sydney hesitated a moment before asking, "Then you would be willing to answer any questions he has? You'd be willing to help him find his sister?"

"Willing? Well, of course I'm willing. What sort of mother do you think I am that I might not be willing to help my sons complete this quixotic quest my husband has sent them on?"

"That's very generous of you. I'll make sure I pass on the message to Griffin." When she could reach him. Where was he?

"Or…" Caro let the word dangle there suggestively. "If you happened to know what he wanted to discuss with me, you could join me for lunch and simply ask me yourself."

"I…" Oh, God. How was she supposed to answer? "I…" On one hand, Griffin was nowhere to be found and, as his mother had pointed out, they were on a time crunch here. On the other, Griffin must have had his reasons for saying he was going to his parents' house and then not going.

Maybe the same reasons he didn't share his schedule with her and made bizarre phone calls that he didn't want her listening in on. If he were a different kind of guy, she might think he was stepping out on her. Maybe she was being naive. Sure, Griffin was a playboy and a charmer, but in the time they'd been together, he'd seemed to curb his outrageous flirting. Plus, the sheer scorn in his voice when he discussed his father's philandering made her think he just wasn't a cheater.

What would it hurt for her to go see Caro Cain and just talk to her? Maybe it would even be for the best. After all, Griffin obviously didn't have a great relationship with her. Perhaps a neutral party could more easily get an honest answer from her.

"I would love to meet you for lunch," she found herself saying.

She quickly jotted down the address, even though she and nearly everyone in Houston knew the location of the River Oaks Country Club.

As she packed up her bag, she even told herself she was doing the right thing. She didn't really believe Griffin would do anything to hurt Cain Enterprises. Not intentionally. But clearly he was not objective here.

Sure, there was a line when it came to respecting a boss's decisions. But if he wasn't available to make the decision, that line was blurry. And if he wasn't being one-hundred percent logical and responsible, then maybe the line even wiggled a little bit.

By the time Griffin pulled up in front of his parents' house, he still hadn't decided what do to about Hope2O. He was so lost in thought he almost didn't recognize the Jaguar XK parked at the curb. Only when he saw the sticker for the rental car company did he remember that the same car had been parked there nearly three weeks ago when Hollister had made his big announcement. Which meant Cooper must be visiting. Of all his father's possible visitors, only Cooper was enough of an adrenaline junkie to rent a Jaguar every time he came to town.

Ever since their father's first heart attack, Hollister had been sleeping downstairs, in the room at the front of the house that had once been his office. Now, all the furniture had been replaced by a hospital bed and enough medical equipment to sustain a surgical ward in a third-world country. Griffin knew this because he'd actually visited clinics in Africa that got by with less.

Today, he peeked into the room and saw that his father was sleeping. He briefly considered waking his father up, but instead he quietly closed the door just as a nurse bustled around the corner. She was one of three who cared for Hollister around the clock. Patting her mouth with a napkin, she said, "I'm sorry, sir. I was just taking a lunch break."

"You don't have to apologize," he assured her. "You're allowed to eat."

The nurse, a pretty woman in her mid-twenties with curves and twinkling eyes, giggled a little. "Thank goodness," she said with a smile.

Instead of hurrying back to her food, she lingered. There was something coy in her posture and expression that let him know that she'd stay and chat if he wanted her to. It'd be easy enough. He could ask how her lunch was, tease her about being away from her station, listen sympathetically about her grueling hours. There'd been a time he would have chatted her up, gotten her number and a few days later probably taken her to bed. There'd even been a time when he would have thought that the break he and Sydney were on meant he was free to do just that. Today, he wasn't the least bit interested.

Instead of flirting with the girl, he just asked, "His condition is still stable?"

Her expression faltered, but she quickly rallied, nodding professionally and saying, "Yes, sir. One of us will contact you if there's the slightest change."

Which answered the question at the back of his mind. She knew exactly who he was—the heir to the fortune. The man with his hands wrapped around a golden ticket.

That was always the problem with women who knew about the money. And, somehow, they always knew about the money. Except with Sydney. Sydney had never seemed remotely interested in that.

He nodded politely to the nurse. "Thanks."

Then he made his way down the hall toward the back of the house, only to see Cooper leaning in the doorway to the kitchen, his hands shoved into the pockets of his jeans and a smug grin on his face.

"Boy, you're slipping." Cooper liked nothing more than to get a rise out of him or Dalton.

"I don't know what you're talking about," Griffin said.

Cooper nodded in the direction of the hall down which the nurse had disappeared. "Come on, a prime piece of ass like that? Normally you'd be all over that."

"I think I have a little more restraint." He couldn't resist adding a subtle dig. "And a little more class."

Cooper pushed away from the door. He flashed a toothy, humorless grin. "Which is your way, I suppose, of saying I have none."

"Hey, that's not what I was saying. But the fact that you heard that is a bit of a Rorschach test of your insecurities, doncha think?"

Cooper had the long and lean build of an Olympic snowboarder, which is precisely what he had been before he started his own company designing and manufacturing snowboards. He was the kind of athlete who was as good in front of the camera as he was on his board. All in all, Cooper was an expert at playing the game, whatever the game was.

Which was one of the reasons why Griffin couldn't get a read on Cooper's mood, not until Cooper was close enough to give Griffin a friendly slap on the arm and say, "So how've you been?"

"Fine." Griffin resisted the urge to rub at the spot on his arm. "So what're you doing here?"

"I just came by to have lunch with the old man."

"He's asleep," Griffin observed.

"He was tired after eating."

Griffin held up a hand palm out. "Hey, I'm not criticizing, I'm just surprised. I would have thought you'd be headed back to Colorado by now. It's been, what, a couple of weeks since Dad's big announcement?"

"I was busy doing…" Cooper's voice trailed off as he apparently fished around for the right word. "Stuff."

"Business stuff?" he asked, even though it was none of his concern. If Cooper could give him a hard time, then he damn well better be willing to take it, too. Besides, if Cooper was also searching for the missing heiress, Griffin wanted to know about it.

"No," Cooper said simply. Then his mouth spread into a wide grin.

"Any chance you're still in town because you're looking for the heiress yourself?"

Cooper's smile broadened without necessarily softening any. "Do you really think I'd tell you if I was?"

No, he didn't. They'd never been close, so why would Cooper share information, even if he had it?

"Are you leaving soon, though?" Griffin asked as Cooper headed for the front door.

"My flight leaves tomorrow morning." Cooper pulled his hand out of his pocket, extracting his keys. He sent a last look back through the door to the kitchen, which he'd just walked through a few minutes ago. "But I'm considering changing my plans. Extending my stay a little longer."

Cooper had almost made it out the front door when Griffin said, "Hey, if you're going to be in town, we should get together." Cooper turned to stare at him, his mouth slightly agape, his surprise so obvious, Griffin felt obliged to add, "You know, hang out or whatever."

That cynical smile flirted across Cooper's lips again. "And not talk about the heiress at all."

Griffin laughed. "Yeah. I can see why the offer looks suspicious. But I mean it. You're not in town that much. Dalton and I don't see you often enough."

"Oh, but you and Dalton hang out all the time?"

"I wouldn't say all the time. But after the divorce he moved into my building, so, yeah, I see him. Not that he'll be around much this week."

"Right. 'Cause of Laney."

Because Cooper had lived in their house for a couple of years after his mother had died, he knew Laney, too, and, as far as Griffin could tell, they'd even been close back in high school.

Cooper had looped his key ring on one of his fingers and he gave the ring a jostle so the keys flipped around his hand and he caught them again. Griffin smiled because he did that same thing with his keys.

"What do you say? There's a great sushi place not far from the office."

Cooper shrugged, though he still looked surprised. "Sure. We should do that."

But, in truth, the invitation had surprised Griffin, too. He'd never before had the impulse to bond with Cooper. Neither he nor Dalton had ever been particularly close to Cooper. Yeah, they'd lived in the same house for Cooper's last two years of high school and during summers before that. They'd wrestled and fought. They'd played touch football more roughly than they probably should have. But had they ever really talked? About anything?

For the first time in his life, that bugged Griffin.

It occurred to him now that once Hollister died, Cooper might never again come down to Texas. Unless there was some major shift in his relationship with his brother, once Hollister was gone, he might never see him again.

Suddenly, he thought of Sydney and all that he'd learned that morning from that damn file. Of the foster mother she still kept in touch with. Of the other kids who'd grown up with her in that foster home with whom she still kept in touch.

It wasn't the kind of thing Sydney talked about. Hell, he shouldn't even know about it, but he did. And he couldn't shake the impression that if Sydney knew just how lazy he was in his relationship with Cooper, she'd be disappointed. Why that mattered, he couldn't say. All he knew was that if Sydney had a half sibling, she'd damn well have done more than have her assistant send a card at the holidays.

He didn't stop to ask himself why it mattered what Sydney

would do. Instead, he followed the faint sound of clattering dishes into the kitchen, where he assumed he would find his mother. Yes, it was rare for her to cook and even odder for her to clean, but he figured that must be where she was because the house was otherwise quiet.

However, instead of his mother, he found Portia at the sink, quietly loading glasses into the dishwasher. Portia had been married to Dalton for nearly a decade before their divorce a year ago. Though Dalton never complained that Portia still flitted about the edges of their family, Griffin found it bizarre as hell.

She looked up when he walked in and gave a jump as if he'd startled her out of deep thought. "Oh, it's you."

He stopped on the far side of the kitchen, not wanting to get too close to Princess Portia. "I was looking for my mother."

Daintily drying her hands on a dishtowel, Portia sighed, making it clear that speaking to him was a burden. "She's having lunch at the country club."

He glanced at his watch. "Perfect. I'll check there."

"You should call first and have her add you to the guest list," Portia said in her most *helpful* voice. "Otherwise they might not let you in."

Like all good Southern women, Portia's helpful voice was designed to eviscerate unsuspecting victims.

"Just out of curiosity, why are you here at all?" he asked. "I mean, you do know that you're not actually part of this family anymore, right?"

Her hands clenched on the towel before she tossed it aside. "I'm here because your parents are going through an extremely difficult time and none of you boys has the common sense to check in on them."

Ignoring the sting of truth that accompanied that barb, he said, "I'm here now."

"And I'm guessing you came to harass your mother about what she knows about Hollister's illegitimate daughter."

"I—"

"She knows nothing. And I can't begin to tell you how distressed she is by this mess that whore stirred up."

The vehemence in Portia's voice nearly rocked him back a step. "Wow, that's an awfully harsh word, Portia. Did it tarnish that silver spoon on the way out of your mouth?"

She ignored his jab and strode forward to the massive island that divided the kitchen and separated them by a good eight feet. She planted her palms down on the granite and leveled a stare at him.

"You may not give a damn about this family, but I still do, even if Dalton and I are not together."

"Yeah, can we circle back around to that? Because I'm still not sure I understand what you're doing here now when you and Dalton are divorced."

"I'm here because Caro asked me to come."

"I had no idea you two were so close." There was a sneer in his voice and he didn't bother to hide it. It irked him a little, that she and his mother were close. Nothing he'd ever done had been good enough for his mother. But she'd welcomed Portia like a long-lost daughter.

Portia must have heard the bitterness in his voice because she shrugged without really meeting his gaze. "Your mother and I have a lot in common. We were both pressured into marriages with powerful men who didn't give a damn about us. I think she admires me for having the courage to walk away. Besides, she was like a mother to me for ten years."

For the briefest moment, he wondered if it really was cowardice rather than greed that had kept his mother by Hollister's side all those years. Then he decided it didn't matter. She could have left. At any point in her thirty-plus years with Hollister she could have walked away. She could have done what was best for her kids and left an emotionally abusive man. Instead, she'd stayed. Maybe it was callous of him, but he resented her for it.

He snorted his derision. "Right. You came running to be

with her because she was like a mother to you for a decade, but that's about ten years longer than she was ever like a mother to me."

Portia's expression softened and she blew out a sigh. "Look, I know she wasn't a perfect mother to you or to Dalton, but try to see this from her point of view. She never asked for this. She's the victim here as much as you, Dalton and Cooper are."

"I'm sure she's hoping either Dalton or I will win the company and throw her a bone or two."

Portia gave him an assessing look. "And will you? If you find your sister, will you give your mother some of Hollister's fortune?"

He answered without even having to think about it. "Yeah. I will. But don't tell her that."

"Her husband is dying," Portia said. "You could show a little sympathy."

"More to the point, her dying husband is cutting her off. If she's crying, I think I can guess why."

Portia stared hard at him and then tossed down the dishtowel she'd held clutched in her hands. "You know, Griffin, you really are a piece of work. You act so superior. You criticize your parents for caring more about money than people, but when it comes down to it, you're scrambling after Hollister's money, too."

"That was the point of this challenge, wasn't it?" Griffin said past the hot knot of anger choking him. "He wanted us scrambling after him."

"Maybe he just wanted your attention," she countered.

"I suppose you think I'm a worthless son for not caring."

Portia shook her head in exasperation. "Look, it's not my business."

"Well, at least we agree on that." He moved to walk out but then stopped at the last minute. "You never told me who she was having lunch with."

Portia had turned away from him to face the sink, and before she turned back he noticed that the tail of her shirt was untucked from her pants. And the twist in her hair had come loose and then been hastily repinned. Looking at her from behind, he realized she was more rumpled than he'd ever seen her. Before he had a chance to wonder why, she turned around and offered him a cold smile.

"I thought you knew. She's having lunch with Sydney Edwards. Your assistant. I'm surprised you didn't know." His shock must have shown on his expression because a broad smile cracked the icy beauty of Portia's face. She looked at her watch with an exaggerated gesture. "In fact, they should be sitting down for lunch right about now."

Eight

Sydney knew she was outclassed the second she set foot in the River Oaks Country Club. Actually, she knew she was outclassed the second she pulled her aging Civic up to the security gate. River Oaks County Club was one of the most exclusive in the country. The sprawling antebellum clubhouse was built of pale bricks, its grandeur reinforced by oil fortunes and a century of social climbing. None of that intimidated Sydney. She'd spent her whole life being outclassed. The way she saw it, in terms of class and social prestige, pretty much everyone was higher on the totem pole than she was. No point in getting upset about that. When it came to interacting with people beyond her means, she was used to faking it.

When the maître d' showed her into the dining room where Caro Cain was already waiting, Sydney had to clench her hands around the strap of her purse to hide the faint tremble in her fingers.

But Caro stood up and, rather than shake Sydney's hand,

gave her an air kiss, which somehow managed to be welcoming and dismissive at the same time.

Taken aback, Sydney awkwardly reached out to return the hug, but Caro had already stepped away.

"Um, thank you for inviting me to lunch," Sydney said.

"Of course!" Caro enthused. "I want to do anything I can to help."

"I see," Sydney said as she lowered herself to the cushioned edge of the seat. The second her bottom touched fabric a waiter was at the table filling up her water glass.

"Would you like a glass of wine?" Caro asked, as though she was a hostess rather than merely another guest at the country club's restaurant.

"Just tea, please," Sydney answered.

Caro gave the waiter a distant smile. "Another wine then for me and a sweet tea for my guest."

"Unsweetened," Sydney quickly corrected her. "I like to keep things simple."

"Very well." Caro nodded. "An unsweetened iced tea," she said to the waiter. Her tone was beleaguered, as if Sydney's choice was a personal affront to her.

"So," Caro said when they were alone again. "Now you're helping Griffin with his search for the girl."

"Yes."

"I'm certainly willing to do anything I can to help."

"Yes, well, the forty-two boxes of household records you sent over have been very informative."

"I'm so glad," Caro said, and though her tone was effusive, it lacked true feeling. "Though I'll admit I was a bit worried about just handing over so much personal information. But I suppose it can't be helped."

Caro gave a fragile smile accompanied by a fluttering hand gesture. Sydney had the odd impression that she wasn't really having lunch with Caro, but rather that she was attending a stage performance. Maybe something by Tennessee Williams, something with a lot of wispy Southern women dripping with family drama. Sydney had never cared for Tennessee Williams. She was more of a Mamet girl, herself.

She couldn't help wondering if Caro Cain was truly as fragile as she appeared. After the waiter dropped off the drinks, Sydney pulled out her iPad and prepared to take notes.

"I'd like to ask you a few questions," she began.

Caro pressed her fingertips to her chest, feigning surprise. "Were the household records not enough?"

"There is a lot of information in those forty-two boxes. Searching through them is quite a job. Because we are a bit short on time, I'm sure you can appreciate the need for efficiency."

Caro delicately brought her napkin up to her eyes as if blotting away fresh tears. "Of course. My dear Hollister could pass at any moment."

The phrase "my dear Hollister" gave Sydney pause, especially after what Griffin had said earlier about Caro abhorring Hollister. *Abhor* was a pretty strong word. And perhaps his failing health had softened her emotions.

"Erm…yes, of course," Sydney hedged, fiddling with the settings on her iPad as she wondered how best to steer the conversation. "If we could just—"

"You don't like me much, do you?"

Sydney snapped her gaze to Caro's face. She cringed. "It's not my place to—"

"I supposed Dalton told you all sorts of horror stories about me."

"Dalton never really discussed his personal life," she was able to say honestly.

"Hmm." Caro took another sip of her wine while pinning Sydney with a cool, assessing gaze. "Then I suppose you've just formed your own opinion based on what you think you know about me."

"I…" Christ, what was she supposed to say to that? "It's really not my place to have an opinion about you."

"Nonsense. Everyone has opinions." Caro waved a dismissive hand and then studied Sydney shrewdly. "I suppose you think I brought this on myself. That I'm as much to blame as Hollister because I turned a blind eye for so many years." She sighed, staring off into space for a moment. "And maybe I should have left, but I knew he loved me in his own way. Hollister is a great man. But even great men never accomplish great things without the right support system. I told myself I could be that support he needed. Perhaps I fooled even myself."

Slowly, Caro's gaze swiveled back to Sydney. Though Sydney met the other woman's gaze, she had no idea what to say. Honestly, she couldn't pretend to be sympathetic, but she also couldn't deny that she understood what Caro meant. Hadn't she just had a similar thought herself at the office? Not exactly, of course. But similar. That's what being an assistant was all about. Taking pride in someone else's work. Helping someone else achieve greatness while being content to stay in the background.

It seemed she could see Caro's faults so clearly, but perhaps that was because they mirrored her own.

Caro seemed to be waiting for some response, so Sydney spoke, hesitatingly at first. "I can't speak to your relationship with Hollister. That's not my place. But I can say this—Griffin also has it in him to be a great man."

"Griffin?" Caro asked.

"Yes, Griffin." The surprise in Caro's voice annoyed her.

"Oh, I'm not disagreeing," Caro added hastily. "I'm just surprised. You worked for Dalton for much longer. I expected you to be touting his greatness."

Heat rose in Sydney's cheeks as she realized her mistake. She had only been Griffin's assistant for a handful of days, and that's how Caro would see it. "Of course Dalton is also great," she fumbled for a response. Something, anything to hide the depth of her involvement with Griffin. "Dalton is incredibly intelligent. And ambitious. And…" Now she was overplaying it. She paused to take a sip of her tea. "I merely meant that I can see greatness in Griffin, too."

"Yes. I agree." Caro leveled another one of those cool, assessing stares at Sydney, giving her the feeling that she'd hidden nothing from the other woman but exposed entirely too much.

"Well," Sydney said with forced confidence. "About those questions I had…"

"Yes," came a voice from right behind her. "I have some questions, too."

Sydney's heart gave a little jump. She knew his voice without having to turn around.

Griffin was here.

She slowly looked over her shoulder. He was standing behind her, just to her right. How much had he heard? More to the point, why was he here? Was he angry with her?

She pasted an ingratiating smile on her face. "Hello, Mr. Cain."

Her use of his last name must have irritated him because his gaze narrowed slightly. "Ms. Edwards," he said with a nod. "Mother." He crossed to Caro's side and brushed a kiss across her cheek. "You look beautiful, as always."

Caro offered him a restrained smile. "Hello, dear. I assume you want to join us. We haven't ordered yet. Shall I have the waiter pull up a chair?"

She was already gesturing when he stopped her with a hand to her arm. "No. Thank you. I'll take Sydney's chair. She can't stay."

"I can't?"

"No. You can't. I need you back at the office."

"You do?" Nice try, but she wasn't going to let him bully her, not when she was just starting to feel like she was making real progress with his mother.

"Yes." He gave her a pointed look. As if she was too dense to get the point. "There's a lot of work to do today."

"Then I'll stay late." She smiled back at Caro. "Your mother was nice enough to invite me to lunch. It would be rude to leave her now."

"You can go back to the office and I'll have lunch with her."

"But—" Sydney began, but then broke off. Glancing back at Griffin, she said, "Perhaps we should discuss this in private."

Griffin looked like he'd rather discuss it back at the office, but instead he gave a tight nod. "Mother, if you'll excuse us?"

"Yes, of course," she murmured.

"Come on, then."

Sydney stood, leaving her shoulder bag at the table because that way he couldn't just show her out. However, instead of taking her out the front of the club, which she'd feared he would do, he guided her out the back, through one of the many glass doors, onto the sprawling patio that overlooked the expansive golf course.

Even though it was late October and theoretically the temperatures should be dropping, it was still in the eighties and the persistent humidity made the air feel sticky. The view of the pristinely manicured lawns of the River Oaks golf course was stunning. It was almost oppressively beautiful. Too beautiful, actually, like the photo on a postcard that's been touched up so much it no longer looks like a real place.

And she knew that was true of the River Oaks Country Club. There was nothing here that was real. Nothing solid. It was all surgically taut skin and chemically brightened grass.

But perhaps she was prejudiced, her opinions colored by her status as an outsider.

Beside her, Griffin said, "Don't pretend you came here to lunch with my mother just to admire the view."

She glanced up at him, taking in the lean lines of his face. Griffin also had that otherworldly quality to him. Not false, exactly, but still too pretty to be real. Unbelievably handsome.

She turned to face him fully. No, she was done pretending. "Of course I'm not going to pretend. I'm here to talk to your mother, just like you are."

"The question is, why are you here when you're supposed to be back at the office?"

"Your mother called *me*. She offered to help in any way she could. I tried to get a hold of you, but you weren't available. When she offered to talk to me instead, I accepted. I wanted to strike while the iron was hot. I didn't do this to undermine you or go behind your back. I was trying to help. That's all."

He opened his mouth, his hand raised like he was about to jab a finger toward her to emphasize his point. Then he snapped his mouth shut, spun around and paced about five steps away. Only to turn back around, fists clenched at his side, and glare at her. "You do not need to be here."

"I feel like she's really starting to open up to me. Maybe I—"

"If you feel like she's starting to open to you it's because that's what she wants you to feel."

"You're saying she's manipulating me?"

"That's what my mother does best." Suddenly, there was no belligerence in his tone. No frustration. Just exhaustion. "Just go back to the office and let me handle her."

She responded with as much honesty as she could. "I don't think I should," she answered simply. "I'm supposed to be helping you find the missing heiress. Your mother obviously has information that we need. If she'll open up to me—"

"We don't know that."

"She must! And I'm sorry, but the fact that you can't see that makes me question your judgment."

"My judgment?"

"Yes, your judgment. This argument we're having is ridiculous. I'm trying to do what's best for Cain Enterprises and I really believe your mother will open up to me. You've admitted to me that you don't get along with her. Maybe I'll have more luck. Shouldn't you at least let me try?"

And this, Griffin realized, was why sleeping with his assistant was a dumb-ass idea.

Marion might be nearing fifty and matronly, she might be a little slow to navigate the latest software and she might even be still reporting to his father—which he'd long suspected, but never had any firm evidence of—but at least Marion followed directions. If he'd sent her back to the office to dig pointlessly through boxes, she'd have done it with a cheerful smile and brought him cookies later.

But no, not Sydney. Because Sydney knew him too well to fall for his bull.

"Look, there is nothing wrong with my judgment. Let me question my mother."

Her brow furrowed with doubt. Hoping to push the argument over the edge, he ran a knuckle across her cheek. Her eyelids dropped a fraction and she swayed just a little. And this was the advantage of sleeping with your assistant. At least when she was as responsive as Sydney was.

"Trust me," he coaxed.

Her eyes snapped open. "Trust you?" She stepped back, putting more distance between them. "I'm supposed to just trust you? That's really rich coming from a guy who won't even let me glance at his Day-Timer."

Where the hell had that come from? "That has nothing to do with this."

Her gaze narrowed slightly. "Try to see it from my point of view. How am I supposed to trust you when you never explain anything? Do you deny that you're hiding things from me?"

He turned away from her and stared out at the lush green lawns of the golf course. He gritted his teeth. "I was just trying to protect you."

"I don't understand…protect me from what?" Her expression was blank with confusion.

"I'm trying to protect you from my parents. They're not nice people," he admitted. "Bitter. Angry. Manipulative. Pits of nuclear waste are less toxic. And things at the house have only gotten worse since this crap with the heiress started. Why the hell would I want to expose you to that?"

He heard her steps behind him, felt the air shift as she propped her hip against the limestone. The rock was cool beneath his palms. Solid and strong. Everything about the country club, everything about this entire neighborhood was designed to convey strength and power. It was designed to intimidate and exclude.

He waited for her to speak, but when she didn't say anything, he finally looked up at her.

Though her body was facing him, she'd turned her head to stare out over the lawn, too. "So you think…what? That she would intimidate me?"

There was confusion in her voice, but also something else. Something he couldn't quite identify. Like she was hurt maybe.

"It's not just you. My mother intimidates everyone. Except for the people she manipulates. One day she'll treat you like she's your best friend, the next she cuts you out entirely. Friendship, affection, love…for her, those aren't emotions, they're currency. It's not that I didn't think you could handle her, but…" He straightened and turned to face her. "You're not used to this world. You grew up in a world where people cared about each other. Took care of each other."

She gave a snort and he instantly regretted his words. Because he now knew that wasn't entirely true. Her own mother was worse even than his. But horrible in a different way. It was only after Sydney had been removed to foster care that she'd had anyone to take care of her. Only then had she lived in a world where people loved one another.

If he'd thought it through first, he would have phrased it

differently, but he couldn't very well apologize now. Not when she didn't even know he knew about her birth mother.

Still, he said, "I'm sorry. I never meant for this to be a big deal."

She cocked her head to the side again. "Then why is it such a big deal?"

He shrugged, suddenly feeling self-conscious. He wasn't used to talking about his family with anyone. He didn't like to play the poor little rich boy card.

"Next time," she said, "if you have a logical reason for doing something, just tell me. You don't have to be so damn secretive about everything."

"Neither do you," he pointed out, thinking about all the things she hadn't told him. Things he knew only because of that damn background check.

She nodded, slowly. "Okay. It's a deal. From now on, we talk more. We're in this together, right?"

"Right." And suddenly, he found himself smiling at her.

Right up until she added, "If we don't get better at sharing information, we're never going to find this girl."

"Right," he said again. Of course that was what she talking about. "Come on, let's get back in there and finish up with my mother."

He walked a few steps before he realized she hadn't followed. When he turned back, he saw her watching him, her mouth twisted into a wry smile.

"What?" he asked.

She gave a self-conscious shrug and crossed to his side. "I've never had anyone try to protect me from anything, even if it was misguided," she admitted in a soft voice. "Thank you."

All he could do was nod because if she knew the truth, she sure as hell wouldn't be thanking him. If she ever found out how much he knew about her past, she'd be furious.

But, as she pointed out, they were only in this together until they found the heiress. After that, all this talking, and sharing and intermingling of their lives would end. So that was something to look forward to. After that, he could go back to having sex with Sydney instead of sharing all this emotional crap.

Nine

Sydney tried to keep a silly smile off her face as she walked back into the dining room to rejoin Griffin's mother. Everything she knew about the woman, everything Griffin had said and her own instincts told her that Caro Cain would not be pleased if she knew her son was involved with anyone's assistant. She was the kind of woman who would want her sons to date and marry debutantes.

Plus, they'd been out on the patio talking long enough that she was probably already suspicious. Despite all that, Sydney was unexpectedly pleased by Griffin's words. They filled her with a warm fuzziness that had nothing to do with the afternoon's high temperatures. By the time she reached Caro's table, Sydney made sure her expression was carefully professional. Polite but distant.

She wished inside she felt the same, instead of the disconcerting torrent of emotions that were rushing through her.

Caro Cain raised her eyebrows coolly as Griffin held out the chair for Sydney. "Well, you were certainly gone a long time. That must have been quite the discussion you had."

"Just some business we had to clear up from the office," Griffin answered smoothly.

"Anything I can help with?" Caro asked.

Griffin offered his mother a tight smile. "Certainly not, Mother. You know how you hate talking business at the table."

Caro sniffed. "As if that ever stopped your father." Then she blotted at her eyes again. She made a sound like a strangled sob. "What I wouldn't give just to share a meal with him now."

"He's not dead yet," Griffin said wryly as he sat down.

Caro's gaze sharpened. "Do not disrespect your father to me."

Griffin shrugged, but Sydney could tell he was about to launch another volley, so she leaned forward and interrupted the familial sparring. "Mrs. Cain, let's get back to those questions I wanted to ask you."

"Yes, of course. But I will say I was surprised that you're working for Griffin now."

Sydney wondered just how much Caro had deduced of her relationship with Griffin.

"Of course I am," she said quickly. "The CEO needs an assistant. And when Dalton left—"

"Yes, of course." Caro smiled benevolently at Griffin. "I'm sure this won't shock you, but I can't say that I'm sorry Dalton has stopped looking for the girl." Caro leaned close and dropped her voice. "If only one of you can inherit everything, then I'd much prefer it be you."

Sydney watched the revulsion flicker across Griffin's face as his mother patted his hand conspiratorially, but Caro didn't seem to notice it.

However, she did turn her assessing gaze to Sydney. "What I meant earlier was that I was surprised you're still involved. If Dalton has indeed left the company, then why are you still around?"

Caro's questions made one thing clear: she was on to them. She may not know for sure that they were sleeping together, but their long discussion out on the balcony—or perhaps her earlier fumble—had tipped their hand. Caro knew something was up.

Before Sydney could answer, Griffin peeled his mother's hand off his arm and said, "Sydney is working for me now. I needed someone to help me transition to interim CEO."

"And you didn't want to bring your own assistant with you?" Caro asked.

"No." With each question, Griffin's tone cooled. "I needed someone who was familiar with every project on Dalton's plate."

Caro's lips turned down in disapproval. "And besides, you've never really trusted Marion, have you? After all, she worked under your father too long for that, didn't she?" Instead of waiting for him to answer, Caro turned her cool gaze on Sydney. "You, however, haven't worked at Cain Enterprises long enough to have any alliance."

Sydney blinked in surprise at the icy chill in Caro's voice. "I don't… I'm not sure what you mean."

Griffin replied instead of Caro. "She's implying that you're not qualified for the position."

Caro's lips twisted in an unpleasant smile. "Nonsense. I'm sure that the only qualification that Dalton cared about was that she had never once worked for his father. Naturally that one quality prepared you for a position of tremendous power within the company. Unless there are other qualifications I'm unaware of."

"Enough, Mother," Griffin said sharply. "That's a line you don't want to cross."

Caro looked from Griffin to Sydney and back again with her eyebrows raised in feigned innocence. "Oh, I'm sorry." She patted the back of Sydney's hand. "Have I offended you, dear?"

Sydney forced a smile past the bitter taste in her mouth. "Not at all."

But she was starting to see what Griffin had meant about his mother.

"Excellent. I knew you were made of sterner stuff. Now, tell me what you need to know that you haven't been able to find out from the files I sent over."

Well, that was tricky because she'd learned precisely nothing from the files at all. In fact, after Caro's comments about Dalton, Sydney was beginning to wonder whether Caro hadn't been deliberately unhelpful before now. After all, she'd just admitted that she wanted Griffin to find the heiress instead of Dalton. Dalton had been the one who had originally requested the household documents be sent over. Perhaps Caro had simply sent over forty-two boxes of useless papers just to waste Dalton's time.

Of course, demanding answers about that would gain her nothing, so instead Sydney said, "I don't know if Dalton explained why he wanted the household records from that time period, but—"

"He did," Caro interrupted with a sweeping gesture. The wine in her glass sloshed precariously. "Something about a nanny."

"Yes." Sydney paused, wondering if Griffin was going to take over, but he remained silent. "Dalton and Laney had a theory about one of Dalton's nannies. Apparently, she worked for you when you were pregnant with Griffin. Her name was Vivian. She was pregnant when she worked with you. And they know for sure the child was a girl."

Caro took another sip of wine and Sydney couldn't tell if she was stalling for time or if she was merely disinterested.

Griffin lost patience with Caro before Sydney did. He leaned forward. "Do you remember the woman or not?"

"Not off the top of my head."

"I have pictures of her, if that would help." Sydney pulled the file from her bag and pushed the pictures across the table to Caro.

Caro glanced at them without a flicker of surprise or recognition.

"Do you know this woman?" Griffin asked.

"Perhaps. I don't know." Caro waved dismissively. "If there was a pregnant girl who worked for us, she certainly didn't stand out. That is the point, isn't it? That they were the help. Good help isn't seen or heard."

Her tone fairly dripped with derision, making it perfectly clear she thought Sydney was well outside her bounds.

Yeah, Sydney got the point. But she hadn't clawed her way out of poverty by feeling the sting of every subtle insult. Caro would have to work a lot harder to scare her off.

Sydney took a long sip of her iced tea. As she set down the glass she said, "You're a smart woman, Mrs. Cain. I can't believe there could be anyone in your home, help or otherwise, who could make a play for your husband without you knowing about it."

Caro's expression froze into an icy mask, and for one long moment she neither moved nor spoke. Then, abruptly, she smiled with smooth ease. "Well, there's your mistake. You seem to be under the impression that there was only one nanny making a play for my husband."

"There was more than one?"

"Of course. They *all* made a play for him. Hollister has always been quite charming. Add in his personal wealth and his power, and he was virtually irresistible. Every secretary at Cain Enterprises, every female geologist in R&D, every young nanny who cared for the boys—every last one of them was susceptible to his charms."

"*Every* single one of them? That's hard to believe."

"Really?" Caro tilted her head to the side, her expression all innocence. "Can you honestly not imagine that a smart and beautiful young woman might try to use sex to align herself with a wealthy and powerful man?"

Aha. And there it was. The cutting jab she'd been expecting ever since they'd returned to the table. Sydney opened her mouth, readying her own defense, but before she could speak Griffin leaned forward. "That's enough, Mother."

Caro blinked innocently. "Excuse me?"

"Enough with the thinly veiled barbs. Do you remember the name of the nanny or not?"

For a long moment, Caro studied her son, her gaze cunning in her assessment. Then she cut her gaze to Sydney for an instant before her lips turned up in a coy smile, leaving Sydney with the impression that Griffin's defense of her had revealed precisely the information Caro had been digging for.

"In the months she worked for us, I barely spoke to her." Now that Griffin had called her on her attitude, Caro's tone was clipped and irritated. She was obviously a woman who liked to play with her food but didn't like it when her food swatted back. "How am I supposed to remember her name?"

Sydney found herself frowning. "You barely spoke to her? How long did she work for you?"

"Maybe five, six months."

"You had no interaction with her in six months? When she had sole responsibility of caring for your children?"

"She was competent and kept the children out of my hair. Why on earth would I speak to her?"

"Because they were your *children*."

Caro just waved her hand dismissively, clearly as disinterested in her progeny now as she had been then.

Sydney glanced at Griffin, expecting to see pain flash across his face at his mother's matter-of-fact dismissal. Instead, his expression was shuttered, his eyes unreadable. If his mother's carelessness hurt him, he didn't show it.

Somehow, his carefully hidden reaction made her ache even more deeply. She didn't want to see him openly in pain, but she would have understood that. She could have pitied that. But this? This emotional distance? This careful detachment with which he held his emotions in check? This was much harder for her to see. Because it was achingly obvious that he had expected his mother's reaction. Not because that was how she really felt, but because she'd obviously crafted the barb to punish him for standing up for Sydney.

And suddenly, she got what he'd been trying to tell her earlier about his family. About how ill-equipped she was to deal with their mind games.

She understood something else, too. He hadn't been protecting only her. By keeping her away from his mother, he'd also been protecting himself. However clever they were at hiding their relationship while they were at work, his mother had seen right through the ruse. She now had information about Griffin that she could use against him. He was now vulnerable to his mother's manipulations. Because of her.

Just like that, all the warm, fuzzy goodness that had been coursing through her veins seemed to seep into her belly and congeal into a mass of nerves.

Despite that sick feeling in her gut, Sydney wasn't going to back down, either. Caro knew more than she was saying. Sydney had no doubt about that.

"Okay," Sydney said, keeping her tone diplomatic. "If you don't remember the girl's name, surely you can think of someone who might. There's got to be someone else who can help us find her. How did you hire the nannies?" Sydney asked. "Did you use an agency of some kind?"

Suddenly, Caro's eyes lit up. "Yes. There was an agency. They sent nanny applications over."

Griffin sat back in his seat and gave Sydney an appreciative grin. "Great. Then all we need is the name of the agency."

"I don't have it."

"You what?"

"I don't have it. But Sharlene Sheppard should. Hollister asked Sharlene to help find the nanny. She contacted the agency herself."

"Okay then," Griffin said, pushing back his chair. "We go talk to Sharlene."

Sydney pushed back her chair and stood. She waited until they'd said their goodbyes to Caro and were out of hearing range before asking, "We?"

"Yes," he said grimly. "In for a penny, in for pound, right? Now that you've met my mother, you might as well meet the rest of the cast in this Greek tragedy."

The whole situation made Sydney sad. She'd always felt like she'd gotten the short end of the stick when it came to family. No father in the picture. A mother more interested in scoring her next hit than in parenting. No extended relatives to take over.

But the tangled mess that was the Cain family made her realize just how lucky she'd actually been. She'd landed with a great foster mom. She had foster siblings she cared about. And at the end of the day, she knew she had people who cared about her. Did Griffin have that? Had he *ever* had that?

She thought not. And it simply made her want to cry.

Ten

Griffin had always loved Greek mythology, particularly Homer's *Odyssey*. That bit about Scylla and Charybdis…that was pure gold. The way Griffin saw it, Homer's family life must have been about as fun-filled as his own because anytime he had to deal with both his mother and his father's former mistress, that's how he felt—like he was trapped with a horrible six-headed monster on one side and a treacherous whirlpool on the other.

Was it any wonder he hadn't wanted Sydney to accompany him through those particular straits? Even Odysseus lost good soldiers on that trip.

Though Sharlene looked like a defenseless waif—much as his own mother did—Sharlene was strong. If Caro's personality sometimes seemed as formidable as a six-headed monster's, then Sharlene was the vortex that unwittingly sucked people in. At heart, Sharlene was nice, a rarity in his childhood, but good intentions hadn't stopped her from creating countless problems and endless grief. He'd spent ten years of his life trapped between Scylla and Charybdis.

When he was a kid, he'd actually preferred spending time with Sharlene. Whenever they'd gone to the offices of Cain Enterprises, it had always been Sharlene who had taken care of them. She'd kept crayons in her desk—a hundred and sixty-four count crayons, too, not the measly sixteen count—and she always made sure she had paper to draw on. And when he'd had an emergency appendectomy when he was seven and his mother was out of town, it had been Sharlene who had stayed with him at the hospital.

Of course, as an adult, he could see that the emotional vortex was its own kind of monster. None of which explained why the thought of seeing her again after all this time made him feel sick to his stomach. But of all the women Hollister Cain had seduced and used badly, Sharlene had deserved it the least.

It wasn't until he'd pulled the car onto the loop and was heading for downtown that he felt Sydney's gaze firmly on him.

He glanced over at her, frowning. "What?"

She looked at him with her head cocked slightly to the side. "You're nervous."

He scoffed. "No, I'm not."

"Really?" she asked, looking pointedly at the spot on the steering wheel where his fingers tapped out a frantic beat.

"Okay." Why had he lied in the first place? So he was nervous about seeing Sharlene again. No big deal. "Maybe a little."

"You want to tell me why?"

No, he didn't.

She shrugged as if she didn't really care either way. "I just thought it might help. Talking it out might make you less nervous. If she's as formidable an opponent as rumor has made her out to be, you might be better off not displaying any signs of weakness."

"Rumor? What rumors?"

Sydney shrugged a shoulder. "I've just heard stuff around

the office. Sharlene Sheppard is now, what? The COO of Sheppard Capital? She's supposed to be an amazing business-woman."

"So?"

"And she's supposed to hate the Cains. And now you're supposed to face her down and try to get information from her? This is like braving the lion in her den. It would be normal to be nervous."

"She's really not like that."

"Are you sure? Because I've never seen you nervous before." Her shoulders shifted as she gave a little shrug. The movement did nice things for the little sweater stretched tight across her chest, but even that couldn't distract him enough to take his mind off her words. "True, we haven't been together that long, but I've never seen anything phase you. When you found out Dalton was resigning and leaving you in charge of a billion-dollar company, you didn't even blink. You faced down the board and convinced them to name you interim CEO and you didn't even break a sweat. Frankly, they were eating from the palm of your hand so contentedly, I think you could have asked them to toss out the interim and just be CEO and they would have done it."

"Your point?"

"My point is, neither of those situations made you nervous." She softened her words with a smile. "But you obviously are now. So I don't really know what to do with that."

"You don't have to *do* anything with it," he muttered, even though he knew it wasn't the answer she wanted.

He was silent for a long time. Long enough for Sydney to give another one of those shrugs and to finally turn and look out the window. Like she'd accepted that he just wasn't going to answer. The truth was, even he didn't think he was going to answer. But then she sighed. The noise was almost inaudible over the sound of the car's engine and the ambient hum of traffic, but he still heard it.

Her sigh was as soft as a whisper but filled with regret.

Before now, their relationship had been perfect. Great sex untouched by complications, free from the angst and anguish that emotional involvement brought to the table. He'd thought Sydney was perfectly happy with that arrangement. Why would she—why would any woman—want to listen to him whine about his past?

But then there was that sigh. That regret-filled murmur that sounded like a trumpet's blare. He hated knowing that she regretted being with him. Hated knowing that she was sitting here in the car, wishing she was with the kind of guy who opened up and talked about his feelings. Never mind whether or not there actually were any guys like that in the world. Never mind that he had never, in any of his previous relationships, been the kind of guy who talked about his feelings.

He didn't like to think that she regretted being with him. So, as he pulled off the highway toward downtown, he admitted, "Sharlene isn't a formidable opponent."

"She isn't?"

"No. Sharlene is—or at least was when I knew her—a genuinely nice person. She's a good woman. And she never deserved to be involved with anyone like my father."

Sydney was quiet for a long moment. When she finally spoke, all she said was, "I see."

He hadn't meant to say anything more than that, but something about Sydney's quiet acceptance made his words come out of him in a rush.

"She was his secretary and his mistress for nearly ten years when I was a kid. Sometimes, during the summer or on school holidays, he'd bring Dalton and I up to his office. She was the one who would keep us entertained. She gave us crayons and printer paper for drawing. She even had a little stash of Brach's candies in a jar on her desk just for us."

"Let me guess," Sydney interrupted. "Peppermints."

He shot her a sideways glance. "The peppermints were for Dalton. How'd you guess?"

"He keeps Brach's peppermints in his desk drawer. I used to think of it as his one human weakness. You know, before he quit his job and ran off to be with the woman he adored." Sydney considered him for a minute. "So what kind did you like?"

"The white nougat ones with little jellies inside."

"I liked those, too, when I was a kid." She nodded seriously. "So if you have all these great childhood memories of Sharlene—and for the record, she does sound pretty awesome—then why are you so freaked out about going to see her?"

"I'm not freaked out."

"You're a little freaked out."

"I'm not—"

"Do you need me to run through the list again of the things that didn't make you this nervous?"

Sydney was looking at him with raised eyebrows and an arch expression. Her tone and words were teasing, but he could see in her eyes that she wasn't about to back down on this. He was struck by the sudden urge to pull over the car and…and what? Demand she get out and mind her own business? Or maybe just kiss her senseless so that they'd both remember where the boundaries of their relationship were. This was supposed to be about sex and pleasure. Not about prying painful childhood memories out into the light.

When he didn't say anything—because, God, what could he say?—she kept talking.

"You know, if it was me, I might feel guilty that my father treated her so badly."

"Who said he treated her badly?"

"I inferred it from the fact that your father hates Sheppard Capital and has tried to destroy them financially. If that's not horrible treatment, I don't know what is."

"Yeah," he muttered, his voice gruff. "Good point."

She had him so distracted he'd actually forgotten the conversation they'd had less than an hour ago. Or maybe he'd just blocked it out. He wasn't used to talking about his family with other people.

"Yeah, that's a nice theory, but I'm well past the age where I feel like I have to justify my father's behavior. He's an ass. There's no point in me apologizing for that."

"And yet you clearly feel guilty for how Sharlene was treated. If you're not apologizing for his behavior, then for whose?" She was silent for a minute, then abruptly she swiveled in her seat so that she was looking at him straight on. "You can't feel badly about how you treated her when she broke up with your father."

He shrugged, not entirely sure what to say, partly because it hadn't occurred to him until just then that he even felt guilty about it.

"She was like part of the family. Like my stepmom or something. Then, all of a sudden, she was gone from our lives."

"You were, what? Nine?"

"Ten."

"Look, Griffin, your father's love life is clearly all kinds of messed up. It was wrong that he had a mistress for all those years and acted like it was normal for her to spend time with you and be your friend. It was wrong for them to put a kid in the middle of all that. You were ten. You shouldn't have even known what was going on between them, let alone felt guilty for not sticking up for her or something."

"Maybe not. But I knew she'd been treated badly. Maybe I shouldn't have done something when I was kid. But I've been an adult now for twelve years. That's long enough that I should have found the time to apologize."

She seemed to be considering him seriously, but then she gave a snort of derision. "If you were acting like an adult at eighteen, then you're a better person than I was at eighteen."

He thought about what he knew about her—the things she'd told him and the things he'd learned on his own. "Yeah, I don't believe that for a minute. At eighteen, you were what? In college, taking eighteen hours a semester and working two jobs to pay your way."

He knew he'd slipped up the second the words were out of his mouth. Suddenly he found himself wishing the traffic would clear. Mere moments ago, he was glad for the traffic because it allowed him to postpone the inevitable. Now he wished he was already there.

She hadn't seemed to have realized his gaff yet, but she was smart and—unlike so many people he knew—she actually listened to what others were saying. He figured he only had a few more seconds before—

"Wait a second."

And there it was.

"Okay, I know I've mentioned college. But I never said anything about two jobs."

He faked causal. "I was guessing. You're not the type who would want to incur a lot of debt. You're not the type who would have let your foster mom pay for you." He glanced in her direction, but her gaze was still narrowed and suspicious. "It was a lucky guess."

"Were you guessing about me having a foster mom, too? If you had to 'guess'—" she made air quotes "—what college do you think I would have attended while I was working these two jobs?"

Five semesters at Houston Community College and another four at the University of Houston. "How would I know?"

"Yeah. That's what I'm wondering. How would you know?"

He kept his gaze on the bumper of the white Ford in front of him. Damn traffic.

After a second, he glanced over at her. "How much trouble am I in here?"

She seemed to be considering him, but there was a playful gleam in her eyes. "I haven't decided yet. I guess it depends on how invasively you've invaded my privacy."

"What would you consider invasive?"

"Well, I know Cain Enterprises did a background check when I was hired full-time. So, did you just abuse the privileges your name offers you and get access to my file?"

"I didn't do it on purpose."

"How do you accidentally read someone's background check?" That teasing light in her gaze had dimmed.

"Dalton had the file in his desk. I saw it this morning. I shouldn't have read it, but I did."

And now the details of her life seemed to have lodged themselves firmly into his brain, even though he'd only read the file once. He'd felt vaguely sick to his stomach. His disgust had been partly aimed at her mother because no one's parent should put their kid through the things Sydney had gone through. But mostly, he'd been disgusted with himself because he should never have even looked at the damn thing. Somehow, despite having been neglected and then abandoned by her mother, despite having bounced around the foster care system before finally landing in a good home, somehow, despite all that, Sydney had developed into a decent human being. And she'd deserved better than to have her past dug up.

She clenched the strap of her purse in her hand. It was a classic navy shoulder bag made of fine leather, just large enough to hold her personal belongings and the company-issued iPad. She massaged the strap with such intensity he half expected to see a wear mark on the leather.

"Do you know about Sinnamon?" she asked abruptly.

"I do."

Sinnamon was the name Sydney's birth mother had given her. Her foster mother had filed a petition to have it changed with she was eleven, which was a few years after she'd ended up with Molly Stanhope.

"Do you know about Roxy?" she asked after a moment.

"Your birth mother? Yes."

"What else do you know?"

"More than I should," he admitted, keeping his gaze glued to that white bumper as if he could will it out of his way. "The background search that Cain Enterprises did was pretty extensive. After all, you were hired to be the CEO's assistant. It doesn't get much higher up the chain of command than that."

He glanced at her, fully expecting her to be angry; instead, she looked a little bruised but mostly curious. "Do you read the company background checks on every woman you date who works for Cain Enterprises?"

"No! Jesus, this was nothing like that. It was a mistake." She nodded slowly, but she didn't lose that hurt look. He was so focused on the background check and her reaction to that that he almost didn't catch it. "Wait a second. What do you mean, every woman I date at Cain Enterprises?"

"Well, you know…" She gave a little shrug and looked embarrassed. "I've seen how you are with women around the office."

"You think I sleep with everyone at the office I flirt with?" He laughed. "I wouldn't get anything done at work."

She pursed her lips as if lost in thought. "What about Jenna Bartel?"

"Down in marketing?"

"Yeah."

"She's happily married with five kids."

"But she's always flirting with you!"

"Well, yeah. Five kids. She's desperate for adult conversation."

"Okay." She seemed to be scrounging for another name. "How about Peyton in HR?"

He nodded appreciatively. "Oh, she's great."

"So you dated her?"

"No, she's a lesbian. And in a long-term relationship."

"Okay, what about Chloe Young in R&D?"

This time he cringed just thinking about the disaster that would be. "She's engaged to Ryan Thomas."

"Really?"

"Absolutely. And he's one of those medieval Ren Faire types. Owns a broad sword and everything. No way I'm messing with that. He'd kill me."

"Hmmm," she mumbled.

"So have I convinced you?"

"Yes."

"The real question is why you needed convincing."

Sydney hesitated. Well, the answer to that was transparent. It was easy to believe they were having a no-strings, just-sex relationship when she thought she was one conquest out of many. She wanted to be the rule, not the exception.

She felt her cheeks turning pink, and she refocused her attention on the bumpy spot on her purse strap.

"I can't be the first woman you've dated who works for Cain Enterprises."

"Why not?"

She blew out a breath of frustration. Why not indeed? Because it implied she was more important than she thought she should be. Because it meant maybe this was something special. And she so didn't need those kinds of thoughts in her head. Instead of going down that twisted path, she asked, "So you've honestly never slept with someone from Cain Enterprises before me?"

He snorted derisively. "I'd have to be an idiot to make a regular practice of it."

"Why do you say that?" Sure, she knew why she thought sleeping with coworkers was a bad idea—despite the fact that she was doing it—but she'd also worked enough places to know a lot of people did it anyway.

Instead of answering outright, he asked, "Do you have any idea how much money I'm worth?" Then he muttered a curse. "Or rather, how much I would be worth if my father hadn't lost his mind."

She didn't know any precise numbers. "Not really. But I can guess, based on what the company's worth and how much stock your father owns. From working with Dalton, I gather that, before your father's little trip to fantasy land, he intended for your mother to get ten percent of the company stock and for each of his three sons to get thirty percent."

Which would officially put Griffin into the crazy, stratospherically rich category. Something that made her really uncomfortable if she thought about it too much.

"Exactly. Everyone I work with can make a guess and get within a couple million dollars of my potential worth. Would you want to date someone under those circumstances?"

"Good point."

"Besides, it's not just the money. If I made a mistake and trusted the wrong person, it wouldn't be just me paying for it. It would be the whole family. The entire company."

She couldn't help asking, "Have you made a mistake like that?"

"Once. I was young and stupid. It could have been a lot worse than it was." His hands clenched on the steering wheel and he gave it a little twist, like he was stretching out his arm muscles while he was trying to decide what else to tell her. "But mostly I just learned from watching the way my dad operated. He had women he slept with all over the world, but he rarely let any of them close. Of course, after Sharlene left him, that's when it got really bad. He didn't trust anyone after that."

"Is that why you think this affair he had with the heiress's mom must have been before he got involved with Sharlene?"

He seemed to ponder that for a second. "Yeah, I suppose so, though I didn't think it through before now."

"Here's what I don't get—I've worked with Dalton for nearly a year now, and I've never seen any indication that he's even half this paranoid."

"He's not," Griffin agreed. "But Dalton's different. It's like what you said about the way he looks at you."

She nodded, knowing what he meant. "Like you're a resource, not a person."

"Exactly." He drummed out another beat on the steering wheel. "It's not even that he really thinks that. That's just the perception he gives. But no one would ever look at Dalton and think that he was vulnerable. If you're going to invade a castle, you don't try to blast your way through the front gate—you look for the weakest spot in the defenses. You try to find the back door and sneak in that way."

"Wait a second. You can't think that's how people see you!"

"Of course it is." He shrugged. "I'm the second son. I've never been a serious contender for power within the company. I don't have a real job there."

Even though she'd had the same thought, she bristled in his defense. "You have a real job!"

"Do I?"

"Of course you do. You're the CEO."

He raised his eyebrows in mocking question. "Really? I've been interim CEO for about five minutes."

"And before that you were a VP."

"A VP of what, precisely?"

"You were the VP of International—" But then her memory failed her and she couldn't remember what exactly he did internationally.

"International…" he prodded.

"International something."

"Any idea what I do—or rather did—as VP of International Something?"

"Well, you…travel a lot. And I'm sure you…have a lot of meetings. And…"

"Come on. Seriously, can you describe my job?"

"Well, no. But I'm sure *you* could."

"Look, I don't do a lot at Cain Enterprises. I'm the first person to admit it. If it wasn't a family business, there's no way I'd actually work for Cain Enterprises."

Interesting. And it made her wonder what he would do if he had picked his own profession.

"But you do actually care about the business. You clearly pay attention to what's going on. Otherwise, you wouldn't have even had opinions about how to handle the change in leadership."

"Of course I *care* about it. If Cain Enterprises' stock tanks, it's my inheritance that goes down the drain."

"That's really what you care about? The money?"

"Hell, yeah."

"I don't believe that." Or maybe she just didn't want to believe it. When he didn't say anything in response, she felt a growing sense of unease. Finally she prodded. "You can't be serious about that."

"Why not?"

"I just don't believe you only care about the money."

"Really? You need me to tell you again how much money it is?" he asked glibly. "Because I only need to care about each dollar a tiny amount for it to really add up."

"You're not that guy. You don't even drive a flashy car. You drive a sensible hybrid."

"Maybe I just care about the environment."

She frowned. Yeah, okay. She could see that. If he cared about the environment and worked for a company that did land development and oil exploration, maybe that was how he balanced it out. "Still, it's a sedan. It's like the least fancy car ever."

"Hey," he said, his voice all mock offense. "Don't diss my car. It's a great car."

"But surely there are other hybrids that are a little more—" she mentally fished around for a word that wouldn't be dissing his car "—stylish."

"Sure. That's why I have a Tesla parked in the garage under my condo, but it's not like I'm going to drive that puppy to work every morning."

She didn't even know what a Tesla was, but she could guess. Somehow, knowing he owned a fancy sports car annoyed her, even if she didn't know jack about fancy sports cars. Even if it fit every preconception she had about him.

Yeah, when she'd first met him—hell, even when they'd first started sleeping together—she'd thought he was just some charming playboy type. But in the past few days, her opinion of him had shifted. And the truth was, she kind of liked the guy who cared more about Cain Enterprises and who drove an unimpressive sedan.

That charming playboy? He was a great guy to sleep with. Fantastic in bed. Loads of fun to hang out with. But that other guy—the guy who worried about the family company and drove a sensible car? That was a guy she could really care about.

Not that she wanted to care about him. That was just a heart-ache waiting to happen.

The truth was, she was perilously close to caring way more about him than she wanted to. The last thing she needed was more reasons to like him.

No matter what else happened, no matter how their relation-ship seemed to have changed in the past few days, it was just an illusion. The relationship had taken on this false sense of intimacy. The no-strings, just-sex relationship they'd started out with four months ago had gotten very muddled. Things went downhill the second they stopped having sex. Now that they were sharing their histories and emotions, this felt like a real relationship. Like something that might last.

But she knew that was an illusion. He needed her right now. His entire life had been thrown into turmoil over the past six weeks. First with his father's proclamation and then again when Dalton quit. Griffin needed her right now because their affair was the last vestige of normalcy in his life.

But she had to be careful. She couldn't let herself forget that this emotional attachment he seemed to feel for her was temporary. Once his life got back to normal, he wouldn't need her anymore. She just had to make sure that she didn't still need him.

Eleven

Griffin couldn't stand the unnatural calm that had overcome Sydney. "You're being awfully quiet."

"There isn't anything to say."

"That sounds like code for you're pissed off at me," he surmised. "You must be mad at me about the background check."

"No. I'm not."

"Of course you are. Why wouldn't you be? I've invaded your privacy."

She tilted her head to the side as she seemed to consider. "Well, yes. I suppose."

He watched her carefully. "So then you should be mad."

She frowned. "Possibly."

"Possibly?"

"Sure."

"Possibly?" he repeated.

"Actually, I'm more than a little curious as to why you want me to be mad." There was puzzlement in her gaze but no real emotion. It was like she was purposefully distancing herself from him.

And frankly, it *did* piss him off. What the hell was wrong with her?

"You want to know why I want you to be mad? Do you have any idea how crappy I felt about reading that file?" They'd finally reached the downtown exit, and he maneuvered the car onto the exit ramp. "The least you could do is be pissed off at me."

She arched an eyebrow, speculation in her eyes. "Let me see if I've got this right…you're mad at me because I'm not mad?"

He fumed for a moment while he formulated an answer. The building that housed Sheppard Capital was only a block off the loop; driving into the parking garage bought him a few minutes. He pulled into one of the visitor parking spots and killed the engine before answering.

"I just don't get it. You should be pissed."

"It's not a big deal."

"It should be."

"No," she snapped. "It shouldn't be. Don't you understand?"

Now her words were laced with the kind of indignation he'd been expecting all along.

"Apparently not."

"That girl that I used to be, that terrified seven year old, she has nothing to do with me."

"I don't believe that."

"But it's true." Sydney flung her car door open and jumped out. She slammed the door shut and waited until he'd climbed out, too, before saying, "That girl, the one who refused to talk to anyone at school because she was terrified that she'd be taken away by Child Protective Services. That girl, who used to Dumpster dive just to get enough food to eat. I am not that girl anymore. I haven't been that girl since I was eleven."

He watched her carefully from across the roof of the car, taking in the steely determination in her eyes, the firm line of her mouth, the furrow of her brow. The gentle slope of her neck, the way her ample chest rose and fell as she sucked deep breaths into her lungs. He might not have guessed she was upset at all, if those deep breaths didn't hint at a racing heart.

Sydney was such a crazy bundle of contradictions. Hard, but not inflexible. Vulnerable, but not weak. And so completely different than anyone he'd ever met.

Her outburst—brief though it was—had told him more about her than any other conversation they'd ever had. As strong as she looked, as smart and competent as he knew she was, he had seen a totally different side of her. He had now glimpsed the child she'd once been. Alone, defenseless and afraid. The idea of that girl was burned into his brain, like the afterimage of a flash of lightning. It streaked across the sky with wicked speed, but it was still strong enough to burn the retinas. The very idea of that young girl was going to stay with him.

And even though he wasn't the kind of guy who coddled his girlfriends, even though he wasn't big on displays of emotion himself, he had the undeniable urge to pull her into his arms and comfort her.

As strong as that instinct was, equally strong was the warning bell roaring in his head that if he so much as tried it, she'd bolt. So instead, he just stood there, waiting for her next move.

Over the next minute, she incrementally got herself back under control. Then she straightened and gave the hem of her sweater a tug. A single strand of red-gold hair had slipped free from the knot at the base of her neck and she tucked it back behind her ear.

Finally, she slung the strap of her purse over her shoulder and headed for the parking garage elevator. "You coming?" she asked over her shoulder.

He nodded, following her. Would she ever stop amazing him? He didn't think so.

The funny thing was, with every other woman he'd ever been with, sex had been the most interesting part of the relationship. But with Sydney he found her as fascinating outside of bed as she was in it. Maybe more.

For a relationship that had started out being just sex, it was getting surprisingly complicated. He had never meant to be this involved with her. He could only hope that because his awful invasion of her privacy hadn't scared her off, then dealing with his complicated family garbage wouldn't, either, because the truth was this new side of Sydney intrigued him. He wanted to see more of her. He just hoped he got the chance to.

As they took the elevator to the tenth floor offices of Sheppard Capital, Sydney was painfully aware of Griffin beside her, watching her carefully. She had the definite feeling that she'd failed some sort of test during their conversation in the car. She didn't know what Griffin had expected of her.

Had he been itching for a fight? Was he looking for a reason to end things between them? She just didn't know.

She honestly hadn't been upset that he'd dug around in her past. She was a little disconcerted about what he'd learned because that was information she didn't share with anyone. Those were things not even Tasha knew about her. She'd worked hard to put that all behind her. It had taken years of therapy to make peace with her past. But she honestly felt like she had moved on. She was a competent adult now. Not that child. No, her life wasn't perfect, but she had a good job—one that paid well and challenged her. She had her own house. She had the stability she'd never had as a kid.

Everything in her life was fine. Fine.

And once they found the heiress, things would go back to normal. They had to because she wasn't sure how much more upheaval she could take.

For now, she just wanted to get through this meeting with Sharlene without incident.

But as the elevator doors opened, she could still feel the tension in Griffin. She could feel him watching her carefully.

To smooth things over, she gave Griffin a playful nudge in the ribs as they walked into the reception area of Sheppard Capital. "Wow. Clearly breaking up with your father was a good move for Sharlene."

"Yep. Unless she preferred to be penniless and powerless," Griffin quipped as he guided her farther inside.

She was acutely aware of the feeling of his hand at the small of her back. Even though he was barely touching her, she felt each fingerprint like it was a brand on her bare skin.

To distract herself, she asked, "What exactly was she doing as your father's assistant that she managed to go from that job to this one? Because suddenly I feel like I'm not pulling my weight."

Griffin chuckled. "Don't worry. I seriously doubt Sharlene had any skills as an assistant that you don't have. But you have to remember Sheppard Capital was in serious trouble when Jack Sheppard died unexpectedly. The company needed anyone they could get. Sharlene stepped in to get it done. I don't think she had any special skills or knowledge. She's the CFO because she's earned it. Because she's fought tooth and nail to keep it going."

"You almost sound like you admire her."

"Almost?" he asked with an arched eyebrow. He then approached the desk of Sharlene's assistant, introduced himself and Sydney and asked to see Sharlene.

At the mention of Griffin's last name, the assistant's lips curled away from her teeth a little, like she found him distasteful, even though she felt obliged to offer him a seat. For the first time since they'd set off on this little adventure, it occurred to Sydney that it might be strange for them to just show up at Sharlene's office without an appointment. It was like opposing armies in a great battle. One didn't just show up in the enemy's camp without first sending an envoy to establish safe passage.

"Have a seat," the assistant said, her voice dripping with disdain. "I'll see if she's available."

In her head, Sydney translated: *have a seat while I verify that my boss would never stoop low enough to see you.*

Just a few days ago, Sydney might have thought Griffin didn't even notice the woman's unpleasant reaction, but she knew him well enough now to realize that he probably did but wasn't showing it.

Sydney stood there, feeling suddenly nervous, knowing that the assistant was no doubt sending an instant message to Sharlene, wherever she was. It was what she had done whenever someone showed up unexpectedly and wanted to see Dalton. It was an easy and silent way to find out if he wanted to see the person or have them sent on their way.

Whatever response Sharlene had given was not what the assistant expected because a moment later she glanced from her computer screen over to them, her expression equal parts confusion and suspicion. Before she could say anything, the door to Sharlene's office flew open.

"Griffin, dear!"

The woman who stood there—Sharlene, presumably— looked to be in her early fifties. She had platinum-blond, carefully styled hair. Everything about her, from her hair to her flawless skin to her elegant pantsuit, spoke of a woman who knew how to take care of herself and spared no expense in doing so.

She took a few steps into the front office, then held out her arms wide. With obvious affection in his expression, Griffin stood, then met Sharlene halfway across the office. Despite the sizable heels on Sharlene's pumps, the woman barely came up to his shoulder.

Sydney was reminded all over again how very tall Griffin was. At just over five-nine, she wasn't a small woman herself, but she'd quickly gotten used to the fact that Griffin was at least five inches taller than she. Griffin was the first man she'd ever dated who had made her feel delicate and feminine. However, beside Sharlene, Griffin looked like a giant. He even lifted her clear off her feet for a moment before setting her gently back to the ground.

Sydney glanced over at Sharlene's assistant, who looked as shocked as Sydney felt by the unexpected display of affection.

Finally, Sharlene released Griffin—but kept a motherly hand on his arm. "Come in, come in."

Griffin started to follow Sharlene into the office, then glanced back at Sydney, giving her a nod to indicate that she should follow.

Sydney watched Sharlene's expression as she rose to follow them. Disapproval flickered over the woman's face but was quickly replaced with a distant but polite smile.

"And you are?" she asked.

"This is my assistant, Sydney Edwards. She's helping me with a project I'm working on."

"Interesting," Sharlene murmured as she gestured toward the love seat and pair of chairs nestled in the corner of the room. "I believe the last time I was over at Cain Enterprises, your assistant was Marion Green. I didn't hear that she'd been let go. What a shame. She was with the company for so long."

Griffin sat in one chair, so Sydney claimed the other. Sharlene sat on the loveseat, crossing her ankles to the side and draping her arm over the furniture.

Griffin smiled, as if he didn't find Sharlene's line of questioning odd. "Marion is still with the company. I suspect that even if we let her go, she'd keep coming to work every day."

Sharlene laughed. "Yes, I suppose so. Well, come in, come in and sit down. My assistant will get drinks. Griffin dear, the last time you visited me at work you were still drinking chocolate milk. Somehow I suspect your tastes have changed. Let me guess." She tapped one perfectly manicured nail against her chin. "Your father was always a Scotch man, but you don't strike me as the type to drink during the day. Shall I have her just bring coffee?"

Griffin nodded stiffly. Sydney got the impression he didn't

want the coffee, but he also didn't want to be rude. He went on to explain the situation with Hollister and his missing daughter before ending with, "We think we know who the woman who wrote the letter might be."

"You do?" Sharlene asked in surprise. "Then you've narrowed it down from a fairly extensive pool."

Griffin ignored Sharlene's comment and said, "We had a nanny who lived at the house from the time just before I was born to when I was an infant. Apparently, she was pregnant and she had some sort of relationship with Hollister. My mother remembered that you helped hire the girl. Or at least found the service that sent her over."

"Hmm…" Sharlene tilted her head to the side and tapped her cheek. "I might have. But I need more to go on than that. What else can you tell me about her?"

"Not much," Sydney admitted. "But we have her photo. Would that help?"

"Certainly." Sharlene smiled broadly.

Sydney pulled the folder out of her bag and handed it to Sharlene, but at that moment, Sharlene's assistant came in to offer drinks, and Sharlene didn't even look in the folder until the assistant had left. Then she made a great show of flipping through the pages within it.

"Is that photo supposed to be in here?" she asked.

"Yes," Sydney said. "It should be on top." She took the folder back from Sharlene, riffling through it herself before admitting, "I'm sorry, the photo must have fallen out in the car. I'll go get it."

Sharlene grabbed her arm. "Nonsense. Griffin was raised better than that. He'll go." A feline smile spread across her face. "Besides, this will give us a chance to talk."

Griffin's gaze narrowed. "Be nice."

Sharlene blinked innocently. "I don't know what you mean."

"She's my assistant. Be nice."

"I'll be fine," Sydney assured him.

As soon as the door closed behind Griffin, Sharlene tilted her head coyly and said, "So. His assistant?"

"Just his assistant," Sydney bit out.

"Oh, my dear." Sharlene laughed. "I know exactly what that means. Don't forget I was just Hollister's assistant for nearly a decade."

"I am truly just his assistant."

"Yes. I'm sure you are." Sharlene's voice dripped with condescension, but there was a knowing gleam in her gaze.

Strangely, it wasn't the condescension that bothered Sydney. It was that look. That look implied a kinship between them. That look implied they were one in the same, both part of the sisterhood of assistant-mistresses.

It was exactly that sisterhood that Sydney had never wanted to belong to. She'd never wanted the kinship or the glimpse into a future filled with bitter resentments.

That look made her all the more determined to convince Sharlene that the relationship she thought she saw was a figment of her imagination.

Needing to convince Sharlene—even if she couldn't convince herself—Sydney gave the other woman the truth. "I've only worked for Griffin for a few weeks. Before that I worked for Dalton. Griffin sort of inherited me. I came with the office."

"I see." Sharlene's eyes narrowed slightly as she studied Sydney.

It took every ounce of self-control she had not to fidget and squirm. Years of being interviewed by CPS officers served her well here. She was used to faking it.

"Well, then," Sharlene said after a moment. "If you know both brothers, all the better."

"All the... Excuse me?"

"You claim you're not involved with Griffin. Despite his obvious interest in you, I might add. Very well. That is your own business. But if you've worked with both Dalton and Griffin, then you suit my needs perfectly."

"Suit your needs?" Syndey sprang to her feet. "Whatever you're—"

"Calm down, calm down," Sharlene cooed, with a dismissive flutter of her hand. "All I need is a little information."

"Information? I will not betray Cain Enterprises!"

"Betray Cain Enterprises? Oh, goodness no." Sharlene gave a trilling laugh. "I have more information on Cain Enterprises than I know what to do with. Corporate secrets are the last thing I need. No, I need information about the boys. Personal information."

"And you think I'm going to give it to you?" The woman was crazy. Stark-raving mad. And quite clever. Sydney could clearly see that Sharlene had gotten Sydney alone exactly for this purpose.

"Calm down," Sharlene said again in that soothing tone. "My interest is not malicious, I assure you."

"Then what is your interest?" Sydney demanded.

"Is it really so hard to believe that I might be curious about them? Concerned even? Are they happy? Is either of them in a well-adjusted, long-term relationship? Is either of them doing what he really wants to do in life?"

Honestly, Sydney didn't know if Griffin was happy. If he was "doing what he really wanted to do in life." So she gave a noncommittal shrug. "Well, who does get to do that?"

"But it's a shame, isn't it? That Griffin's stuck at Cain Enterprises, when that's not what he really wants to do."

"And I suppose you know all about what he really wants to do."

Sharlene gave a self-effacing shrug. "I wouldn't say that I know all about it. I contribute enough to get the monthly newsletters but not so generously as to attract anyone's attention. And I can tell he's not spending as much time as he wishes he could down in Africa."

"What?" Okay, maybe she was just really tired, but the con-

versation seemed to have gone off road into the realm of very
bizarre. "Newsletters? Africa?"

"For Hope2O."

"What?" Sydney said blankly.

"Hope. 2. O," Sharlene repeated slowly. "The international
aid organization Griffin runs."

Twelve

"The what?"

Sharlene recoiled slightly. For the first time since Sydney had walked in, she got the feeling that Sharlene wasn't putting on a show. Her surprise was as real as Sydney's shock. "He didn't tell you?"

"Tell me what? That he apparently runs an international aid organization in his spare time? No. He didn't mention it." Sydney could hear her voice getting all shrill and squeaky. "I'm sorry. Can we backtrack a bit? Start at the beginning maybe?"

Sharlene blinked rapidly. "Yes. Of course." Then she stood and crossed to her desk and began to rummage around in her file folders in one of her drawers. "A few years ago…or more than a few now, I guess, Griffin got involved in an organization called Hope2O. They provide assistance to impoverished villages that are trying to start up water districts in Africa and Central America. They help with organization and arrange financial backing."

"And Griffin is involved in this?" Again her voice sounded squeaky.

Sharlene looked up. "I'm sorry. This has come as a shock to you."

"I just…I had no idea."

Sharlene must have found what she wanted because she straightened and walked back around the desk. She held out a glossy, tri-fold pamphlet. "Griffin is not just involved. As of four years ago, he's their major financial backer. In addition to being on their executive board."

"Of a charitable organization."

"Yes."

"In Africa."

"Yes."

"And he came to you asking you to donate?"

Sharlene gave a trilling laugh. "Oh, goodness no. As far as I know his involvement in Hope2O is his most closely guarded secret. I doubt any of the Cains know about it. Certainly no one at Cain Enterprises knows, but I just assumed you'd have to know about Hope2O, being as close to him as you are. It appears I really was wrong about your relationship with Griffin."

Sydney gritted her teeth, but didn't comment. She refused to confirm or deny Sharlene's suspicions.

"Then how do you know?" she asked instead. Was Griffin really so close to Sharlene? He'd given Sydney the impression that he hadn't seen Sharlene in years.

"I found out about it purely by accident. A few years ago I was having lunch with some of the women I'd worked with at Cain Enterprises. Griffin's assistant happened to be there and she complained about how difficult it was to manage his schedule. How secretive he was. How he appeared to spend far more time vacationing than actually working. This description of him seemed very unlike the boy I'd known. So I looked into the matter."

Sydney didn't know what to say. She was all too familiar

with complaints made by Griffin's former assistant. He was difficult to work with. He did have a reputation for playing more than he worked. But she had just assumed that was who he was.

"You looked into the matter?" Sydney repeated dumbly.

Sharlene sighed, a sound full of guilt and regret. "I know I shouldn't have. I should have trusted that the Griffin I knew as a boy would grow into a decent man. More than decent, in fact. Extraordinary. But I didn't trust what I knew of him. I nosed around in his business and uncovered just how generous and selfless he is. Believe me when I tell you that I'm not proud of myself for doubting him."

Sydney tried to squelch the sick feeling in her stomach. Sharlene felt badly? That was nothing compared to how Sydney felt. Sydney hadn't just doubted that Griffin might be generous and extraordinary. She'd fully believed he was a self-absorbed playboy. She'd slept with him—for months—without ever knowing the person he truly was.

Finally, Sydney willed herself to take the pamphlet that Sharlene was holding. She glanced down. There was a logo at the top of the page, with the word *Hope* and the letter *O* written in nice big letters and the *2* done in subscript, the way you'd write the chemical name for water. Beneath was a picture of a beautiful young African girl carrying a jug on her head along with the statement "Women spend 200 million hours a day collecting water." She flipped open the pamphlet, not reading it, just letting it soak in. Not really believing that Griffin would have anything to do with this organization.

It was too noble a cause for her charming playboy to be involved in. Too far outside the realm of their lives. She could picture him attending charity galas at the country club dressed in a tux, but not drilling water wells in Africa.

Then on the back, she saw it. A picture of a ribbon-cutting ceremony somewhere. In the background, standing just behind the man cutting the ribbon, was Griffin. The picture was small and cluttered with people. If she didn't know every line of his face, she wouldn't have even recognized him. But she did.

Sydney flipped through the pamphlet again, her eyes scanning all the words without really reading them. She looked for any reference to Griffin at all. Any mention of Cain Enterprises. She wasn't particularly surprised when she found none.

Still, when she looked up, she couldn't help voicing her question. "Why would he keep this such a secret?"

Sharlene sighed. "Why does anyone keep anything a secret? I suspect he's ashamed of it."

"Of doing charitable work? It's not like he's a drug addict. He's not laundering money or hosting dog fights."

"Yes, yes, for someone like you or me, charity is a virtue." Sharlene shook her head. "But in Griffin's world, wanting to help others is a sign of weakness. One that Caro and Hollister worked hard to stamp out of her boys from a very young age. Griffin especially."

"Why Griffin especially?"

"He was always much more sensitive than Dalton. He cared about other people. I remember once, in the mid-eighties when the famine in Africa was getting a lot of coverage in the news, Griffin had the nanny bring him up to the office so he could talk to his father. He asked Hollister why they couldn't just give all their money to the people in Africa. I never heard Hollister's full answer because he shut his office door, but by the time Griffin left, he was in tears. Caro was furious. She fired the nanny the very next day."

"That's awful."

"It was. And whatever Hollister said to Griffin, it must have made an impact because I never heard him talk about helping other people again until I found out about Hope2O."

Sydney tried to imagine what Hollister must have said, but she couldn't. Griffin had only been a child. In the mid-eighties, he would have been six or seven. Eight or nine at the oldest.

That was awfully young to have human compassion stamped out of you.

She glanced up to find Sharlene watching her. "Why show me this?" She waved the pamphlet between them. "Why tell me this at all? What do you want from me?"

"I would think that's rather obvious."

"Well, it isn't. Either you're still hiding something or you've gone to a lot of trouble to satisfy your curiosity."

"Fine," Sharlene said, staring across the office to look out the window. "When I was with Hollister, Griffin was like a son to me. So was Dalton, for that matter. I genuinely care about both of those boys, but when things ended with Hollister, he cut me out of all their lives. I've tried to keep tabs on them, but they're both very private men." Sharlene turned her gaze back to Sydney. "Is it so hard to believe that I simply want to know whether or not Griffin is happy?"

For the first time since walking into the office, Sydney felt as though Sharlene was truly being honest. As though she was seeing the real woman beneath the facade.

"No," she answered honestly, sitting back in her seat. "No, it's not so hard to believe. So why not just ask him?"

Sharlene laughed bitterly. "It's been nearly twenty years since I've seen Griffin. Do you honestly think he'd just talk to me? That he wouldn't be as suspicious and guarded as you've been? More so, even."

Sydney didn't know how to respond to that. Two weeks ago, she would have said that Griffin was an open book. That there were no hidden depths, no deep secrets. The perfect wild-oats guy.

Now she knew differently. She'd never met a book more tightly closed or carefully locked. Now she knew the truth. She'd never known the real Griffin. He'd never once showed her the man he really was.

Well, she could hardly blame him for that. She'd kept her

share of secrets herself. The problem was, his secrets concealed the man he truly was.

Four months ago, she'd gotten involved with a jet-setting playboy. A man who delighted in physical and sensual pleasures but seemed to care about little beyond his own amusement.

In the days since becoming his assistant, she'd realized that man was an illusion. The illusion had tempted her body. The real man beneath tempted her heart, her mind. Her very soul. She could fall in love with a man like Griffin Cain.

"I'm sorry."

Sydney looked up to see that Sharlene had come to sit beside her. Sharlene placed a gentle hand on Sydney's arm. Her lovely face was creased with lines and revealed a concern that was almost motherly.

"Pardon?" Sydney asked, not sure what exactly Sharlene was apologizing for.

"I didn't mean to drop this bomb on you. Honestly. I assumed he'd told you about Hope2O. He seemed so protective of you. You seemed so close. I just thought…" Sharlene's voice trailed off, and for a second she seemed near tears herself. "Well, I know what it's like to love a man who doesn't let you in."

"I—" But Sydney cut herself off. Maybe it was easier to let Sharlene believe she was hurt by Griffin's inability to trust her with the truth. It was an explanation that Sharlene would understand, whereas the truth—her fear of loving Griffin—was something she barely understood herself. Finally, she said simply, "Yes. It is hard."

And it wasn't even an outright lie because nothing about this situation was easy.

Fortunately, she was saved from having to say more because Griffin walked back in. She wanted to curl up inside herself and hide. Instead, she had to sit there and sift through Sharlene's conversation for clues to the identity of this girl. She *so* didn't want to be here anymore.

"Did you find the photos?" Sydney asked to hide how disconcerted she felt.

"No. I didn't. I searched the entire car. We either lost them or accidently left them with my mother."

"Oh, look." Sharlene pulled some papers out from between the cushions of the love seat and held them out toward Griffin. "Is this them?"

He glanced at the photos as he took them from her. "Yes. Surprisingly, this is them," he said wryly.

"Well, then," she said as she took them back. "Let me have a look."

Sharlene held both photos, looking from one to the other. After a few moments, she crossed to her desk and put on a pair of discreet reading glass, then flicked on a desk lamp and studied the pictures under the light. After a moment, she nodded, flicked off the light and returned to the seat, handing the photos back across to Griffin.

"So?" he asked, obviously choosing to ignore her blatant manipulation. "Do you recognize the woman? Or the girl?"

"Of course I do. The woman is Vivian Beck. She was Dalton's nanny and yours, too, after you were born."

"Are you sure Beck was her last name?" Sydney asked.

Sharlene's smile cooled as she returned Sydney's gaze. "Quite."

"What else can you tell us about her?"

Sharlene thought for a moment and then shook her head, either feigning regret beautifully or perhaps truly sorry that she couldn't help more. "Nothing. But you should talk to your mother about this. Surely she knows more."

"She said she didn't remember the woman at all."

Sharlene arched an eyebrow in apparent surprise. "Really? I find that hard to believe."

"Why's that? She was pregnant with me and claimed she

barely had contact with her. She thought Vivian might be the woman's first name, but she seemed to know nothing else about her."

Sharlene's mouth curved into an unpleasant smile. "Well, isn't this just like old times, what with your mother's selective memory and her transparent attempts to control everyone?"

"Sharlene, if you know something, just tell me now." Griffin's voice was terse, his impatience obvious.

"Well, it's interesting, isn't it? That your mother claims to barely remember her."

"Why is it interesting?"

"Well, because she simply *must* remember her. She came to the office to see Hollister after she fired the girl. She was furious. Practically hysterical."

If Caro was really that upset about it, then wouldn't Hollister remember the event, too?

Griffin must have been thinking the same thing because he leaned forward and asked, "Did she actually see my father? What did he have to say?"

"She never saw him. He had meetings all that day, but I mentioned it to him." Sharlene smiled mischievously. "But perhaps I downplayed it a bit."

"So he never even knew what happened?" Sydney asked.

"Oh, of course he knew. Everyone at the company knew. People gossiped about it for months. The police were called. There's no hiding something like that."

"The police?" Griffin asked. "Was she violent?"

Sharlene waved a hand. "Oh, no. Nothing like that." She cocked her head to the side, her expression a mixture of curiosity and sorrow. "Your mother really never told you about this?"

Wincing, Sydney glanced at Griffin. Not surprisingly, Sharlene's sympathy—faked or real—only made this worse for Griffin.

"Can you just tell us what happened?" Sydney asked.

Sharlene smiled vaguely. "Of course. The police were summoned because Caro insisted the girl had stolen something from the house when she left. I think your mother knows who the girl in that photo is just as well as I do, but she just didn't want you to know that she knows."

"Back to the nanny. She stole something?"

"Yes. Caro was livid. She'd fired the girl the day before, but when Vivian left she took something of Caro's. As soon as she discovered it was missing, she stormed down to Hollister's office and demanded I help track her down. I tried, but none of the contact information I had worked. Caro claimed I was to blame because I'd recommended Vivian."

"Do you remember what she stole?"

"A ring. Caro's wedding ring, if I remember correctly."

"What?" Griffin asked, leaning forward.

"Excuse me? She stole Caro's wedding ring?" Sydney asked at the same time. She didn't bother to keep the shock out of her voice. She'd faced Caro down and knew how formidable the woman could be. And she wasn't exactly a fluff ball herself. She couldn't imagine having the guts to steal Caro's wedding ring. "I mean, that's hard core. Who would do something like that?"

Griffin blew out a breath. "I think the bigger question is, why would my mother let her get away with it?"

"She did try to look for the girl," Sharlene pointed out with an elegant shrug. "But I don't think she looked that hard. Caro's wedding ring was not very remarkable. It had been in Hollister's family for generations. It was a simple gold band with a few unimpressive diamond flakes. I'm sure if it had been Caro's engagement ring, they would have called out the national guard. Frankly, the weird thing isn't that Caro didn't get the police involved—it's that Caro even noticed it was missing."

"Still, it was her wedding ring. Don't you think that's bizarre?"

Sharlene smiled coyly. "Of course I do. It's bizarre enough that I remember the incident after all these years. I think the real question you should be asking yourself is why Caro claims she doesn't remember it. It's obvious to me that your mother is lying to you."

Thirteen

The charming playboy had vanished.

He was gone. Completely.

Which she should have been okay with. After all, it wasn't as though she actually wanted to talk to him herself. She was too emotionally fragile for that. Too vulnerable.

Still, Griffin's silence unnerved her. He had said absolutely nothing since they'd gotten back in the car. She didn't ask where they were heading. She didn't have to. He was whipping the car through the streets of Houston like a stunt driver on a closed course.

Clearly, he was pissed that his mother had manipulated him. Hey, Sydney couldn't blame him for that. By the time he pulled onto the loop at about sixty, she figured she had to say something.

"Do you think that—?" she began.

"No. I don't." His tone was hard as nails and his gaze didn't even flicker from the road.

"Maybe you should wait until—"

"No."

"Look, I know you're upset, but—"

"Give it a rest, okay?"

She twisted in her seat to face him. "No, I'm not going to give it a rest. Pull over."

"What?" Finally, he looked at her. Just shot a glance in her direction, but at least he was loosening his death grip on the steering wheel.

"Just get off the highway." When he didn't so much as turn on his blinker, she added. "Look, you're pissed off. I get it. You're in no shape to drive, let alone talk to your mother."

"I'm fine." But then, as if to prove his point, a car darted in front of them and he had to slam on his breaks. Muttering a curse under his breath, he eased his foot off the gas.

She watched in silence as his hand twisted on the steering wheel.

"I'm not…" He broke off, muttering another curse.

He didn't finish the sentence, but he didn't have to. She could think of about ten different ways to finish it for him. He was not fine. He was not ready to talk about it. He was not nearly as in control as he wanted to be.

Tension practically radiated from him. His control was whisper-thin and it was all she could do not to rub her hand across his thigh. To try to soothe him. Maybe she would have if she hadn't feared that he would snap altogether.

He flicked on the blinker, eased across the road and a second later exited the highway and pulled into the mostly empty parking lot of a strip mall near the off-ramp. He parked at the back of the lot, under the shade of a sprawling oak. He killed the engine and just sat there for a moment, his hands clenched so tightly around the steering wheel, she thought it might snap under the pressure.

She watched him struggling for a long minute, trying to give him the space he needed to process everything they'd learned in the past few hours. Obviously, his mother knew who the girl's mother was. She'd known and she'd deliberately misled them. Caro Cain's behavior was incomprehensible to Sydney. She couldn't imagine why the woman would purposefully throw roadblocks into Griffin's path, but she did know this. As frustrated as she was with Caro's behavior, it had to be a hundred times worse for Griffin. Who didn't want this job or this responsibility in the first place. Who had been sick of his family's manipulation before this even started.

And the truth was, she didn't know what to say to make any of this better. She didn't know if there was anything she could say to make it better. So instead of trying, she reached out and put her hand on his leg. She felt the muscle twitch beneath her palm. His hands stilled on the steering wheel. Every muscle in his body seemed to freeze. Then he slowly turned and leveled a gaze at her.

She felt stripped bare by the intensity of his Cain-blue eyes. Naked and vulnerable. Completely at his mercy.

"Griffin, I—"

Before she could finish the sentence, before she even knew what she was going to actually say, he threw open the door, unclicked the buckle on his seat belt and propelled himself out of the car.

"Damn it," she muttered before fumbling with her own seat belt buckle and scrambling out of the car.

She rounded the hood and just stood there for a minute, watching as he paced restlessly. He traversed the distance from the car to the tree and back again in long, restless strides. He clenched and unclenched his hands as he prowled, giving the air of a caged beast. But where the panther in the zoo was trapped by the fence and the electric current pumped through the wires, he was confined by his anger.

"Griffin, this isn't as bad as it seems."

He whirled to glare at her. "Are you kidding? I always knew my family was a mess of crazy, but this? This is beyond crazy."

"You don't know that." Yeah. Maybe he did know that.

Maybe it was as bad as it seemed, but she figured, for now, her best bet was to get him calmed down before he did something he really regretted.

"What? You think this isn't bad? You think there's any scenario in which my mother deliberately lied to me, deliberately misled me that's not bad?"

"I didn't say not bad, I just…" Damn. She didn't know what the right response was here. All she knew was that if Griffin went to see his mother now, he'd say or do all kinds of things he regretted. "Look, no matter how bad it is, confronting her now gets you nothing."

Finally, he stopped pacing and whirled to face her. He stood, stone-still, maybe ten feet away, and just stared at her.

Suddenly nervous, she babbled, "I'm just saying maybe you should wait a bit. Calm down first."

"What exactly," he said slowly, his voice pitched low, "do you recommend that I do instead of confronting my family?"

His gaze was hot enough to damn near burn the clothes right off her body.

She swallowed hard as a shiver skittered across the surface of his skin. "Um…maybe some yoga?"

"Yoga?" He gave a bark of laughter and a smile spilt his face. It was a fierce and wild smile, but at least he no longer looked like he wanted to rip something apart with his bare hands.

"Like, meditate or something," she suggested, even though she knew meditation was the last thing on his mind.

He stalked slowly toward her. "I'm not really the type."

She swallowed again, but it got harder and harder to do past the lump her pounding heart had pushed up into her throat.

Oh, dear, she was in so much trouble here. Because, obviously, Griffin wasn't the type. She doubted he'd ever meditated a single instant of his life. He wasn't a guy who could sit still at all, let alone meditate. The only time she'd seen him relaxed—ever—was in bed. And only after they'd both climaxed more than once. Even sex he treated like an Olympic-level sport.

She should not be thinking about sex right now. They weren't supposed to be sleeping together anymore. She couldn't sleep with him, because… Why was she supposed to be holding him at arm's length again? Oh, right. He was her boss. Her boss!

And she was already dangerously close to getting her heart broken as it was.

She needed to remember that. Because after a week of being in his company nonstop, she was like an addict jonesing for a hit of Griffin.

Even though he was the last thing she should have, he was still what she wanted. What she needed.

Geez, she needed to check herself into some sort of rehab program. She just couldn't imagine twelve steps of any kind that would give her the ability to walk away from him.

She couldn't even think when he was looking at her like this. She glanced around, hoping to spot something to distract them, but they were essentially alone. This end of the parking lot was empty. Cars zipped by on the access road without slowing down enough to notice two people talking under a tree. "Um…what were we…"

"About to do?" he asked, his voice pitched low and seductive.

"No." The last thing they needed was to do something. "Talking about. What were we talking about?"

He smiled like he knew exactly what she was thinking. And he probably did. "You were telling me how to meditate."

"Right. Meditate. It's really not that hard. I hear… Um, I think you need to visualize a happy place."

He stopped a fraction of an inch away from her. So close she could feel the heat sparking off his skin. "Okay," he murmured. "Some place happy. I've got a place in mind already."

His lips twitched into a smile and she felt the last of her reserve of willpower melt away.

When he reached for her, she went right into his arms. He buried his hand in her hair as she tipped her mouth up to meet his. Despite the teasing smile that had been on his lips just moments ago, there was nothing light or playful about his kiss. His lips were firm against hers. His mouth hot. His hand possessive. His body hard.

He kissed her as though he needed her desperately. As though there was nothing else in the world but her. As though he was trying to sear this moment into his memory forever, just as it would be seared into her.

She felt the back of the car bump against her legs. She arched against him, opening her mouth even wider as his tongue slipped in to brush against hers. Then his hands were on her hips and he was lifting her up onto the trunk of his car. She wrapped her legs around his waist, pulling his groin against hers. Even through his jeans and her pants, she felt the length of his erection. It was perfect. Divine.

They seemed perfectly fitted to one another. He rocked against the very core of her and pleasure rocketed through her body, making her tremble. Her hands greedily tugged at his clothes, hungrily trying to find bare skin. He pressed her back down onto the trunk of car, following her inch by inch until he was lying fully on top of her. She bucked against him, desperate to be closer.

She felt his hand slipping up under her sweater and her back arched up off the car.

"Wait," she gasped out.

He stilled instantly. Then he groaned and dropped his head down to her collarbone. She felt his breath hot against the skin of her chest.

"Please don't tell me to meditate."

"No. I just think we should go slowly."

He chuckled. "Yeah. Me, too." Then he pulled up, bracing his forearm beside her head as he looked down at her. "But you're right. We can't do this here."

"What?" But then his words sank in. He was right. They

were in a parking lot. A parking lot, for goodness' sake. And it was the middle of the day. "Right. Not here."

He smiled, a slow, sexy smile that showed off his dimples. Obviously he loved having her this disconcerted. She might have been annoyed with him, but she was too distracted by the heat pounding through her.

He levered himself off her and pulled his iPhone out of his back pocket. "Give me ten minutes to find a hotel nearby."

She put a hand on his arm to get his attention and pointed at the nearby building. "You don't have to look far. There's a hotel right here."

It took less than ten minutes for him to get a room. He had her wait in the car—thank goodness because she wasn't sure she'd have been up to the embarrassment of getting a hotel room in the middle of the day. Within fifteen minutes, he was swiping the pass key and letting them into the room. He was kissing her before the door even shut behind them.

He spun her around, pulling off her clothes as he walked her backward toward the bed. His hands were greedy, desperate even. It seemed he couldn't get her naked quickly enough. He yanked back the covers. She kicked off her shoes just as he pulled her pants off her legs. Then he knelt in front of her, first rubbing his cheek against her bare belly, inhaling deeply, like he needed the very scent of her. Then he parted the curls, burying his face between her legs. Pleasure coursed through her body, making her legs wobble beneath her. Weak-kneed and trembling, she tumbled back onto the bed. He followed her, devouring her with greedy strokes of his tongue. Her climax rushed through her, pushing her over the edge as she screamed out his name.

It took him mere seconds to strip completely and then he was on top of her. He plunged right into her, moaning her name, raining kisses on her skin. His intensity overwhelmed her. His desperation thrilled her.

He made love to her like he never had before. Every other time they'd been together, Griffin clung tightly to his control until the last second. He was a master at driving her to distraction while remaining in control. It made him an incredible lover, but she always felt at a disadvantage.

But not this time. This time, he couldn't get enough of her. He couldn't control himself.

Pounding into her over and over, he cried out her name, burying his face in her neck. His need was palpable. He didn't just want her. This was more than mere desire. He needed her. Desperately. And that thought alone sent her tumbling over the edge again as he thrust into her one last time.

Even as she was crying out, she was also crying. Tears streaming down her face because at last she understood. She couldn't have him. She couldn't keep him. And it had nothing to do with the fact that he was her boss. It had nothing to do with work at all.

She needed him to need her. No one had ever needed her before. Not really. And she wanted that—no, needed that— more than she'd ever realized.

And that was precisely why she had to walk away.

He may need her now, but this was only temporary. Of course he needed her now. His life was in turmoil. Everything he knew or thought he knew had been overturned. She represented the last remnant of the life he'd lived before all this nonsense had started with the missing heiress. She was like a security blanket.

Until this moment, she hadn't realized how desperately she wanted him to need her. But now that she did know, now that she understood, she had to get out. Because even if he needed her now, he wouldn't need her forever. But she…she would always need him. Because she loved him.

Only a few minutes later, Griffin rolled to the edge of the bed and sat there, elbows on his knees, head in his hands for several minutes without speaking. Finally, she wiggled up behind him and placed her hand on his back. He flinched away from her touch, stood and stalked over to where his jeans lay on the floor near the door and yanked them on.

"Griffin—" she began.

He looked at her. For one long moment, his expression was completely unreadable. He studied her with such intensity that she slowly sat up, crossing her legs and tucking the sheet up under her arms. "What?"

He crossed back to the bed, sat on the edge and cupped her face in his hands.

"Sydney, I'm so sorry."

Disconcerted, she pulled back, smoothing down her tousled hair and tucking it behind her ear. "Why are you apologizing?"

"I promised you we wouldn't sleep together while I was your boss and—"

"You didn't really promise," she hastened to correct him, trying to lighten his mood. "You scoffed at the idea and tried to control your laughter."

"I knew this wasn't what you wanted. I betrayed your trust."

He looked guilt ridden. Tormented.

A few weeks ago she would have assumed this was all an act, but now she knew better. Now she knew that despite everything, despite his upbringing, despite the arrogance that was so much a part of him, despite his natural charm and easygoing nature, he was an astonishingly decent man. Maybe even the most decent man she knew.

She understood that now in a way that she could not possibly have understood a few weeks ago. Or even twenty-four hours ago.

It nearly broke her heart to think that—in the middle of all he was going through—he was worried about whether or not he'd betrayed her trust. With all he had on his plate right now, with the fate of a billion-dollar company resting on his shoulders, with his family life in turmoil and with his dreams of running Hope2O at risk, he was worried about her. Because that was how compassionate he was. It awed and amazed her. It humbled her.

Pulling the sheet with her, she climbed onto his lap, straddling him. She kept the sheet wrapped around her, so that the only thing separating them was luxuriant cotton. Thin though the barrier might be, she needed it because without it, if they were skin to skin, they would be too close. Pressed against his body, her words would get lost in the intimacy. It would be too easy for this to become about sex. Besides, she'd be too vulnerable.

Instead, she cupped his jaw in her palms and tilted his face so he met her gaze. Beneath the remorse in his eyes, there was the spark of heat. The passion that was always so close to the surface. The passion that had distracted her far too often from the man he really was.

"You didn't betray my trust," she said soothingly. "This was what I wanted. It was what we both needed."

He studied her for a long minute before nodding slowly. His arms snaked around her, one behind her neck, the other cupping her buttocks. He pulled her closer, but rather than kissing her, he bumped his forehead against hers.

"I'm still sorry. I—"

"It's okay." But she could see that the regret in his gaze was still there. The lingering doubts. "I get it," she reassured him. "You don't want to be that guy. The pushy obnoxious guy who manipulates and controls people to get what he wants. I understand now why you don't want to do that. It's because you don't want to be like your father. But trust me. You're not that guy. You're nothing like your father. You're nothing like anyone in your family. I—"

"You're wrong," he said sharply. Then he stood abruptly, picking her up and turning around to deposit her on the bed before pacing over to the sliding door that overlooked the balcony. "I'm more like my father than you know. I have lied to you. I've misled you."

Her heart seemed to catch in her chest. For a moment, she wondered if this had something to do with Hope2O, but he was so serious, so distraught, she couldn't believe that it did. Then she forced out the word, "How?"

Instead of answering outright, he kept talking as if he hadn't even heard her question. "All this mess in my family, this stupid quest our father has laid out, this complicated web my mother has woven, all of it could have been avoided if they would just tell the truth. If just one person in the family would stop lying about everything, would stop trying to manipulate and control the situation to get what they want. If either of them had been honest about anything, their marriage would have been different. I don't want any part of their legacy of lies and deceit and one-upmanship."

She climbed off the bed, wrapped the sheet around her body like a toga and crossed to stand right behind him. The view out the window overlooked the parking lot and the downtown cityscape. She wasn't worried about anyone seeing her because during the day it would be nearly impossible to see into the hotel room from outside, even if there were buildings nearby.

She didn't say anything, but just let him talk. Whatever lie he'd told, whatever deception he'd perpetrated, she didn't believe it was as serious as he was making it out to be. She knew him too well now for that.

"I want to be totally honest with you." He turned around to face her. His hands were propped on his hips, his jeans slung low with the top button undone. His head was slightly ducked, so she almost couldn't read his expression. "I don't have any intention of staying on as CEO for Cain Enterprises."

"I know. You never claimed you did."

He let out a faint groan of frustration. "No. I mean, I've never really had any intention of even working at Cain Enterprises. I've been trying to get away from it since I accepted the job when I was twenty-four. The only reason I even took the job is because my father threatened to cut me off if I didn't work for Cain Enterprises for at least a decade."

"Yes." Again she cupped his cheek. "I know. It doesn't take a genius to see that you're not really happy at Cain Enterprises. You clearly don't fit there. That's why—"

But before she could admit to knowing about Hope2O, he cut her off. "No, it's more than that. It's not just that I don't want to work for Cain Enterprises." His expression still looked so miserable. "It's that I have other plans entirely. Things I've put on hold for the better part of a decade because—"

Finally, she couldn't take anymore of it and she pressed her fingers to his mouth. "I know."

"You—"

"I know about Hope2O."

"—don't… Wait." His eyes scanned her face. "You know about Hope2O? How could you possibly know?" He took a step back, his expression suspicious. "How did you find out? Did Dalton know?"

"Relax." It was all she could do not to chuckle at his open skepticism. "It's nothing nefarious. Sharlene knows. She told me." He was still eyeing her suspiciously, so she quickly explained about the conversation she and Sharlene had had while he'd been off looking for the photos.

The tension seemed to drain out of him as she spoke. Finally he said, "You're not mad?"

"I found out you're generous and charitable. I learned you're doing great things to help all of mankind. Why would that make me mad?"

Worried, yes, because this was the kind of man he was. The kind who worried that his good deeds would be held against him.

"Some women would be angry that I misled them."

"You never misled me. You're just very guarded. There's a difference."

"Well, you say that now. You might feel differently when you've had time to think it over. After all, you started dating a rich man who was in line to inherit hundreds of millions of dollars. Not a man who works for an international aid organization."

"You can't honestly believe I was dating you for the money. That's not the kind of relationship we had anyway."

He shot her an odd look at that. "No. I don't suppose it is."

There was a note of finality in his voice, like he'd reached some sort of decision. Whatever it was, she wasn't sure she wanted to hear more. She couldn't take any more glimpses into his soul. She already felt as though she'd flown too close to the sun.

Fourteen

Maybe he was an idiot, but he didn't figure out something was wrong with Sydney until after they'd already checked out of the hotel and he'd driven her back to her little bungalow in Montrose. As much as he wasn't looking forward to confronting his parents, he knew he had to talk to them and had just assumed that he and Sydney would go as soon as they left the hotel. However, once he saw her clothes, he knew that wasn't an option. Dirt from his car was smeared across the back of her pale slacks and tan sweater. He'd thought he kept his car pretty clean, but apparently he was going to have to talk to the car care service he used.

Sydney was so quiet on the drive to her neighborhood that he had to wonder if something was wrong. When he pulled up in front of the house, Sydney said, "I'll just be a minute. You can wait in the car if you'd like."

"No, I'll come in," he said, not realizing at first that maybe she'd been asking him not to come in.

She opened the front door and gestured him through. It led

straight into a small living room, with an office off to the right and the kitchen straight ahead.

"Help yourself to a drink," she said, hurrying past the kitchen and gesturing toward the refrigerator. She darted into the bedroom, shutting the door behind her, leaving him standing in the living room staring blankly at the door through which she'd retreated, wondering what was up. She normally wasn't shy. She'd dressed and undressed in front of him countless times in the past four months. So why had she shut him out of the bedroom? Was she mad about the whole sleeping-with-her-boss thing?

He hadn't really thought about it when he'd had her spread out over the hood of her car. If he had, he probably would have assumed that she was fine with it. After all, she'd been the one to point out how close they were to the hotel.

While she changed, he occupied himself by looking around the tiny house. It was a bungalow probably dating back to the 1930s or so, but it had obviously been updated. The kitchen was open and modern, with a large granite-topped island floating between the living room and the kitchen. The office probably could have been used as a bedroom, but she had lined the wall with bookshelves and placed an Eames lounge chair in the center of the room. A large brown tabby cat sat curled up in the chair. When he reached out to touch it, the cat opened one eye and growled ominously.

He'd only been inside her house a handful of times, but he knew where it was because he'd picked her up there. It was decorated in mid-century modern antiques, with lots of pale wood and sleek lines. The furniture had all been lovingly cared for and looked like it might have been inherited from grandparents, though Griffin now knew it had not been.

He crossed back to her bedroom, leaning against the frame of the closed door. "I didn't know you had a cat," he called.

"Um…yeah," she called from the other side of the door. "That's Grommet."

"Like the animated dog?"

"Yeah." She opened the door. Now she was dressed in slim blue jeans and a moss-green knit sweater. "Just like that. He likes cheese."

Sydney tugged at the hem of her sweater and didn't quite meet his gaze. She looked beautiful, as she always did, but this outfit was more casual than her normal, middle-of-the-work-day professionalism.

"You ready?" he asked.

She knotted her fingers together, her expression twisting in indecision. "Here's the thing. I don't think I should go."

"What? You can't let them intimidate you like—"

"No!" she hastened to reassure him. "It's not that. I just…" She blew out a breath and seemed to be searching for words.

Sydney, who was never at a loss for words, suddenly was. Moreover, she seemed a little lost in general.

He crossed over to her, cupping her cheek in his palm and tipping her face up to his. "Hey, what's up?"

"I just think that maybe you need to do this alone."

He frowned. She still wasn't quite meeting his gaze and if she bit down any harder on her lip, she was going to start bleeding. He traced his thumb across her lower lip, gently freeing it from her teeth. "No. I need you there with me. I need a voice of reason. I need someone who's not emotionally involved. That's what you said, remember?"

"I know that's what I said, but I'm not…" Finally, she forced her gaze to his. "I don't think I can be your voice of reason anymore."

He thought of how crazy and messed up his family was. He thought of everything his father and his mother had put him through in the past few days. Hell, his entire life. And every time he'd fought them on anything, he'd done it alone. He'd never once, in his entire thirty years of life, had anyone been completely in his corner. Until now. Until Sydney.

She was everything to him now. No matter what else happened he was going to make damn sure that he didn't let her go.

He closed the distance between them and kissed her, molding his mouth to hers. Pouring into that kiss all the things he wouldn't be able to tell her until all this trouble with this family was resolved.

He lifted his mouth from hers and waited until she opened her eyes before saying, "I still need you there. No matter what."

They found his mother at the house, sitting beside his father's bed, reading him the business section of the newspaper aloud. The home health care nurse was sitting in the hall, giving them privacy. Thank God for small blessings. Most days, it was damn near impossible to have a private conversation with his parents; Griffin was relieved that today he'd have a shot at it. He went into the room where his father's hospital bed had been set up. Sydney was beside him as he walked up to the door, and she gave his hand a little tug. With a tilt of her head, she indicated she would wait in the hall, but he didn't release her hand, instead pulling her in with him. Caro sat in a wingback chair between the bed and the window that overlooked the front lawn. The head of Hollister's bed had been raised so he, too, was sitting upright.

Griffin wasn't sure if Sydney had ever even met his father, but if Hollister's fragile appearance shocked her, she didn't let on. Having her by his side, Griffin saw his father through new eyes, taking in all the things he hadn't noticed the past few visits. Hollister's skin looked pale and paper thin. His eyes were sunken. The myriad tubes and IVs hooked up to him only made him look more frail.

But Griffin didn't let that moment of empathy stop him. He marched into the room and tossed the photos of the mystery nanny down on the bed between his parents.

They both looked up at him in surprise, barely glancing at Sydney where she stood in the doorway.

"What is the meaning of this?" Caro asked, her voice cool.

"I was about to ask you the same thing," Griffin replied.

Hollister reached out a trembling hand and picked up the picture closest to him. He made a *harumphing* noise and then let the picture drop. "Is that the best—" his words were cut off by a series of hacking coughs "—you can do? A thirty-year-old picture?"

Griffin stood at the foot of his father's bed, his hands propped on his hips, staring down at his parents. There was a slight tremble in Caro's chin and she appeared to have lost all the cruel bravado that had carried her through lunch.

He felt only the slightest twinge of remorse. He didn't want to do this, but he wasn't the one who had started this, either.

"This thirty-year-old-picture is of the woman I believe wrote the letter. Dalton believed it, too. She worked here as a nanny when I was an infant. And I refuse to believe that neither of you remember anything about her. Especially since she appears to have stalked Hollister and stolen a family heirloom. Mother, if Sharlene is to be believed, before this girl—Vivian—disappeared forever, she had you so worked up, you demanded that Sharlene call the police and have her arrested. The idea that neither of you remember her at all is so preposterous as to be laughable."

For a long moment no one spoke. Hollister was glaring at Griffin, and the enmity in his gaze was strong enough to abolish the illusion that he was a fragile man. Caro had gone as white as Hollister's hospital-issued bed linens.

Finally, Griffin said, "I want some answers, and you should think very carefully before you give them. Because these may be the last words you speak to me."

Hollister gave a snort of disbelief. Caro's hands twitched nervously on the newspaper, causing it to rustle. Then she carefully folded the paper up and stood, placing it on the seat of the chair before crossing to look out the windows at the sprawling green lawns.

"This is all your father's fault."

"Of course it…is," Hollister gasped out through his coughing. "You always bl-bla-blame me. For everything."

Caro threw back her head and laughed. A desperate, maniacal laugh that seemed to echo through the room. "That's because it is always your fault. But this time especially." She spun to glare at her husband. "Why couldn't you just let it go? Why couldn't you just get the letter, feel the gut-wrenching sense of betrayal and just accept the fact that there's someone out there you don't have under your thumb? That's what you were supposed to do, damn it!"

Hollister looked at his wife, blinking in surprise. For the first time—maybe in his entire life—his expression wasn't arrogant and defiant. Instead, it was confused. "What do you mean?" He coughed again. "What I was supposed to do?"

And suddenly, Griffin got it. He understood what should have been glaringly obvious right from the very beginning. All the tension washed out of his body and he bent his neck, dropping his head forward and shaking it back and forth. "Mother, what did you do?"

"Caro?" Hollister asked, his voice sounding strangely hollow.

She turned back to the window, wrapping her arms tightly around her thin body, which suddenly looked frail, too. "I never meant for any of this to happen." She sent a pleading look over her shoulder at Hollister. "I just wanted to punish you. To hurt you like you'd done me so many times. And I knew it would drive you crazy, not knowing more about your daughter."

"So you sent the letter," Griffin said flatly. He stared at his mother, but for a long moment, she said nothing at all. Finally, he closed his eyes and scrubbed a hand down his face. "For the love of God, can't you be honest about at least this? Can't you—"

"I did." Her tone was as flat as his. "I never imagined what he would do. I never dreamed it would come to this."

"But when it did, when he first called us all into this room, showed us the letter and lay out the challenge, why not just come clean then?"

She whirled back to face them, her expression desperate. "Because I'd lost everything! He had cut me out of his will already. All I had was the hope that you'd find the girl, get everything and take pity on me."

"Mother, you—"

"Do you have any idea how hard I've worked trying to get you clues? How hard it was to keep Dalton off the right trail? How complicated this has been to try to feed you information without revealing how much I knew?"

Caro's voice was rising steadily toward hysteria. Griffin just stood there, shaking his head slowly back and forth. He was so tired of his mother's manipulations. If just once she'd stood up to Hollister, maybe he could feel more sympathy for her. But over and over again, he'd watched his mother sacrifice her pride, her dignity and her children to her own greed. She would never stand up to Hollister because doing so might jeopardize the status quo. Even this one tiny rebellion she'd tried to hide and bury beneath a wealth of lies. Another woman would have divorced Hollister long ago, but Caro was either too proud or too greedy, Griffin wasn't sure which.

Hollister's expression had sharpened into bitter distaste. "Caro, you ignorant twit," he said.

All three of them turned and stared at him. It was the same phrase the letter had used, and Griffin felt another pang of sympathy for Caro. No matter how manipulative and mean she might sometimes be, she didn't deserve to have her husband speak to her like that. Ever. Let alone in front of her son.

Griffin turned his back on his father and spoke to his mother, his voice softer now. "Mother, is there any truth to the letter at all? Does Hollister have a missing daughter, or did you just make it all up?"

Caro clenched and unclenched her hands in front of her

chest, the tears in her eyes now spilling over. "Vivian really was Dalton's nanny. She really did give birth to a girl and I believe that girl is Hollister's child. Why else would Vivian have been so obsessed with Hollister? Why else would she have taken his mother's ring?"

"She could have just been angry that you fired her. Did you think of that?"

"No," Caro shook her head. "If you're angry, you take something valuable. You steal a thousand dollars' worth of silverware that no one will notice until Christmas. You take the five hundred-dollar bills off the dresser. I wasn't wearing either ring that day. She overlooked my engagement ring with its eight-thousand-dollar diamond as well as probably ten grand in other jewelry, all so she could take Hollister's damn heirloom. That's either stupid or crazy."

He turned back to his father. "Okay then, it's on you. Did you sleep with that young woman?"

Hollister didn't even look at the picture. "Of course I did. But Vee turned out to be crazier than a June bug in July. Following me back here. Hiring on as the nanny. I refused to see her."

"So this girl, Vivian, Vee, you never even knew she was pregnant, did you?"

"If I had known, do you think we'd be having this conversation now? But don't you start thinking you've won, buddy boy. Identifying the mother was never what this challenge was about. I don't care who sent that letter." His long speech caught up with him and he once again dissolved into a fit of coughing. When he spoke again, his voice was thin. "You have to find the girl."

"No. No, I don't." Griffin looked at his father first and then back to his mother, once again shaking his head. "But if Cooper wants to, this will give him a place to start."

"What are you saying, boy?"

"I'm out," Griffin said simply.

"You're what?" Sydney asked. It was the first time she'd spoken in the entire conversation and everyone looked at her. Caro still looked tearful and broken. Hollister looked like he hadn't even realized she was there. Griffin turned and smiled at her.

"I'm done. Just like Dalton. I'm done looking for the heiress. I'm done working for Cain Enterprises. I'm tired of being a part of this sick, dysfunctional family. So I'm done." He walked back to where Sydney stood beside the door and held out his hand. She put her hand in his automatically, even though she knew she couldn't hold it long.

"Come on," he said. "Let's go."

She let him lead her out of his parents' house. He moved so fast it was like he was fleeing.

She stumbled along, taking three steps for every two of his. He knew he was walking too fast for her, but he also knew she'd be able to keep up. And he just wasn't willing to stop until they were well clear of the house, crossing the lawn back to his car. Then she dug in her heels and tugged her hand from his.

"Wait. Griffin, wait."

Griffin turned to look back at Sydney, half expecting to see that she'd stopped because she'd lost a shoe or something. But instead, she was just standing there under one of the sprawling live oaks that draped over his parents' lawn.

"What?" he asked. He wanted to keep moving. To get into his car, slam it into gear and tear down the highway. It was the same adrenaline fest he'd experienced earlier today, but instead of being fueled by anger, this time it was the sweet heady buzz of freedom.

Sydney took a step back from him. Almost as if she was afraid of him. "You're making a mistake."

"What?" This time it was flat-out confusion. What did she mean *a mistake?*

"Giving up on the search. Quitting Cain Enterprises. It's a

mistake. You need to go back in and tell them you've changed your mind."

He let out a bark of laughter. "Are you crazy? Did you hear that conversation in there? I'm not going to change my mind. I quit."

"You can't quit. You can't leave Cain Enterprises."

Sydney held her breath, waiting for Griffin's response. She knew it wasn't going to be pretty. He was hurt. He was angry.

But instead of taking out his anger on her, he gave a bark of laughter. "Hell, if Dalton can quit, I can quit."

"You may not realize it, but Cain Enterprises is who you are. What would you do if you quit?"

"Who cares what I do? We'll leave. We could travel. Go anywhere we want. Get married. We could—"

She held up her hands, cutting him off. "Whoa, whoa, whoa. Wait a second. Now you want to get married?"

He stared at her blankly for a second, and she had to wonder if he even realized he'd said it. But then he shrugged. "Sure. Let's get married." He smiled, but there was a frenzied look to his expression. "Don't you get it? I don't have to be part of that family anymore. I don't have to be a part of that cycle of misery anymore. I can do anything I want. I can marry anyone I want."

Oh, crap. This was worse than she thought. She had fully expected him to cling desperately to their relationship out of familiarity. She'd been prepared for that. She had not seen this coming. It simply hadn't occurred to her that he would try to sweep her up into his rebellion against his family, but that's exactly what he was doing. Irony of ironies, suddenly she was *his* wild oats.

Which was not at all the same thing as being the love of his life. Despite him proposing to her in what she could only imagine was a fit of delirium, he hadn't once mentioned love. And why would he? Sure, they'd been sleeping together for months, and sure, she had a key to his apartment, but neither of those things signified any real emotion on his part. Both the sex and the key were just accidents, really.

If she was a different kind of person, if she wasn't someone who needed to be needed, she might risk it. She might agree to marry him, hoping that later he'd fall for her just as hard as she'd fallen for him. But Sydney Edwards—Sinnamon Edwards—desperately needed to be loved. Really and truly. Loved for who she was. And so she couldn't risk it.

But she also couldn't tell him that, because Griffin was smooth and smart and if he thought she needed the words to convince her, he'd probably say them.

"You can't run away from your life like that," she said instead.

"Why not?" He held her at arm's length, studying her face as he asked, "What's holding me here?"

"Your job, for starters."

He looked surprised, then suddenly distrustful. "You care so much about my job?"

"Yes. I do. I care about Cain Enterprises. You do, too. You're just too stubborn to see it." She seemed to have his full attention now, so she spoke quickly, not wanting to lose this chance to convince him. "All this time you've been searching for the heiress, planning on hiring Dalton back as CEO, and you haven't seen that you would actually be just as good a CEO as he was. Better, maybe."

He dropped her hands and stepped away, leaving a gap of several feet between them. When he spoke, his voice was flat and devoid of emotion. "So, what? You think I should just stay here. Find the heiress. Stay on as CEO. Then we'll get married?"

She ignored his comment about getting married, because this time it felt more like a jab than a proposal. "What's important is that you find your sister. You have this idea in your head that you can run away to Africa and reinvent yourself, but you can't. You think that the only way you'll ever know that someone loves you for you is if you give up all your money. But that's ridiculous."

"Is it?" His voice was chilling and as lifeless as a block of ice.

"Yes. You are who you are, regardless of whether or not you have the money. And if you walk away from everything now, you're only robbing yourself of the chance to be the person you were meant to be."

"And who's that? Someone with a lot of money?"

"Someone who might have a sister out there who cares about him. Someone who is a great CEO. Think about all the people who work at Cain Enterprises who you know and care about. Jenna and Peyton and Marion. Are you really just going to walk away from them? You're just going to abandon the company? You're really going to do that?"

"So that's your big plan for the future. We keep searching for the heiress. I stay on as CEO of Cain Enterprises." Suddenly, as he spoke, his meaning was blaringly obvious. The fog had cleared. "And you'll be right there by my side. Because, presumably, once I'm worth close to half a billion dollars, you'll get over this fear of being the EA who sleeps with her boss."

Okay, so he wasn't playing dumb, he was being dumb.

"You think I'm after your money?"

"Oh, I think you win either way. You've said all along you were in this for job security. So either you get to stay on as the assistant of the CEO of a company or you end up married to the CEO. Either way, your financial security is pretty much guaranteed, right?"

"That's what you think?" she asked. "That all I care about is the money?"

"Why else would you be so damn desperate to convince me to find the heiress and to stay on as CEO?"

"Because I want what's best for you, you dumbass. Did it

honestly never occur to you that I just wanted you to make the best decision for you?"

"No. That never occurred to me. And you wanna know why? Because if you do know about Hope2O and you really understand what I'm trying to do there, then you'd understand that nothing would make me happier than funneling all that money into a worthy charity."

"Oh, I understand all right." He made her so mad, she wanted to launch herself at him and strangle him. Instead, she satisfied herself with merely stalking across the pristine lawn and getting right up in his face. "I understand perfectly well that your family has you so emotionally messed up that you think no one will ever love you for yourself alone. So you think the only way to earn redemption or respect is to pour all your money into a worthy cause."

"I don't—" He made a meager protest, but she didn't let him finish.

She was too furious to stop midrant. "I get that. And that would be so convenient for you, wouldn't it? Because then when someone fell in love with you, it would be just you on the table. And you'd never have to wonder whether or not they really loved you. And you would never have to suck it up and just learn to trust someone on their own merits. That would be perfect for you, right?"

He was stubbornly silent, refusing to acknowledge the truth to her words.

So she went on. "And maybe that would have worked out for you if your father hadn't come up with this damn contest for Cain Enterprises. But he did and it screwed up all your plans. Because regardless of whether or not you want to admit it, you care about this company. You care about these people. And if you walk away from it now, you will end up regretting it forever. You know what will happen if you don't play Hollister's game, don't you? Cooper doesn't want Cain Enterprises. He has his own empire to run. So Cain Enterprises will end up reverting to the state. Sheppard Capital will probably swoop in and dismantle it bit by bit."

"Cooper—"

"I'm not done yet," she interrupted him again. "Yes, you'll know that whatever woman you end up with down the line will really love you for you—you will damn well guarantee that because you'll both be living in sub-Saharan Africa on the salary of an international aid worker. But guess what? To guarantee your personal happiness you will have sacrificed the jobs and livelihoods of countless people you really care about."

Finally, finally, she was done with the barrage of anger that had rushed out of her. Her! Sydney, who never lost her temper. Who had never been angry at him, not even when he'd told her about the background check.

But she'd lost her temper now because he was being so damn dense about himself, about what he really needed.

And now he just stared at her, like she'd lost her ever-loving mind. So she asked, "Are you really going to sacrifice all of Cain Enterprises, just so you can have some sort of guarantee that you're loved? Are you really willing to make that sacrifice?"

"What if I am?"

"Then you're not the man I thought you were."

"And let me guess…if I am that guy, if I'm that guy who can walk away from millions of dollars, then you don't want to be with me."

"The money is not what I want. It never was."

"Answer the question, Sydney. If I walk away from Cain Enterprises, I lose you. Do I have that right?"

"That's what you don't get. You never had me to begin with."

"You sure about that? 'Cause I'm pretty sure I had you just about an hour ago."

"Nice." She laughed bitterly, even though she wanted to cry. "If you can't win an argument with logic, then throw sex back into the mix, just to make me feel cheap. You know, for someone who doesn't want to be cruel and manipulative like your family, you do a damn good job of it."

"Well, then, you're going to love this. You don't want to be the girl who sleeps with her boss to get ahead. Fine. You're not that girl anymore. You're fired."

"I guess I should have seen that coming. If you can't have what you want, then you'll damn well make sure no one else does, either." She let out a bitter laugh. "You know, if I thought you could actually get away with that, I'd sue you. I think we'll both be better off if we just pretend you never said that." She turned and started to walk away, but then turned back around and looked at him. "You want to know the real reason I would never marry you? Because you're wrong—it doesn't have anything to do with the money or whether or not you get control of Cain. It's because I saw this coming from a mile away. I knew from day one that eventually you'd get bored or frustrated and you'd push me away."

"So you pushed me away first? You just conveniently waited until I let all that money slip through my fingers before doing it."

By now she was so annoyed with him that she couldn't even respond, so she circled back around to him trying to fire her. Even though she didn't really believe he'd do it. Even though she would sue his pants off if he followed through, she couldn't believe he'd threatened it. "Besides, you know the one thing you've forgotten? You can't fire me. You already quit. You're not my boss anymore."

"Oh, I've only told my parents I quit. I'll sure as hell stay on at Cain Enterprises long enough to make sure you never work there again."

"So you'll put up with something you hate just to make me miserable?" She swallowed the welling of grief that swelled up in her throat. "Your father would be so proud."

Fifteen

She thought Griffin would come after her.

Even after all the horrible things they'd said to one another, even though her heart felt like it was being crushed under a steamroller, she honestly expected him to come after her. Even if for no other reason than the fact that she was on foot, miles from home, in River Oaks, for goodness' sake.

He didn't come after her.

He just let her walk away. Which took forever. Just walking down the block seemed to take an eternity. The whole time, she was painfully aware of him still standing there on his parents' lawn, hands fisted on his hips, watching her walk away.

Of course, she didn't turn around and check to see if he was still there. For all she knew, he may have gone back inside and poured himself a drink. But she never heard his car take off, and he never passed her on the road. So the whole interminable time she was walking past the six sprawling estates on his parents' block, she pictured him standing there behind her, watching her walk away.

That image was the only thing that kept her from crumbling to the ground in tears. Because no matter what else happened, she would not let him see her crying. It wasn't strength that kept her going. It wasn't even pride. It was pure stubbornness. He'd crushed her, but she'd been crushed before.

That was the thing about a kid like her. She'd lost everything at the age of seven. Everything she'd ever known had been ripped away from her, even though everything she'd ever known was absolute crap. But once she'd lost everything, she knew she could live through losing everything again. She might have been terrified, but she had just kept going.

So now she kept walking. Just putting one foot in front of the other until she'd finally reached the end of the block. Then she turned the corner and walked some more. Cars drove past without noticing her—not Griffin's car, but others. It was the people on foot who worried her. Twice she saw other women walking on the other side of the street. Once, it was a nanny pushing a high-end stroller that she was pretty sure cost more than her car. The second time a pair of spandex-wrapped trophy wives. Neither spared her more than a passing glance and she turned another corner. Only then did she admit that she was lost. In addition to being emotionally adrift, she actually had no idea how to get herself home.

She wandered down the block for a few minutes before stopping in front of a house with an impenetrable line of privacy shrubs hiding it from the street. Near the street, the branches of a massive live oak dipped low to the ground. She sank to the ground in the shade of the tree, grateful to be at least somewhat shielded from anyone passing by. Then she dug out her phone and pulled up the maps app. She dropped a pin at the current location and then asked for directions back to her own house. Three point eight miles. It might as well be twenty-three point eight. Yes, it would be possible for her to walk home from here, but she just didn't have the energy. She called Tasha.

"Hey, what's up?" Tasha asked. "That lazy boss of yours isn't sick again, is he?"

Sydney had intended to calmly ask for a ride home, but the instant she heard Tasha's voice, the whole story poured out.

"I'm going to kill him!" Tasha said indignantly when the story petered out. "I'm actually going to kill that jerk."

Despite herself, Sydney let out a strangled laugh. "I don't think—"

"No. Really. I think we should kill him. Between you, me, Marco, Jen and George, that's what…five of us who grew up in the foster care system before ending up with Molly. Surely one of us knows someone who grew up to be a professional hit man, right? I'm guessing Jen. She was always the toughest."

Again, Sydney laughed. "Yeah. It would probably be Jen. But don't call her just yet. What I could really use now is just a ride."

Tasha snorted. "Honey, I got in the car as soon as you called. I'll be there in fifteen minutes."

Thirteen minutes later, Sydney climbed into her foster sister's beat-up Chevy. Tasha wrapped her in a brief hug before putting the car back into gear. Tasha was a crappy driver who talked too much with her hands. This was probably the first time they'd ever been in the car together that Sydney hadn't spent the whole drive fearing for her life. Today she simply felt too numb.

For the first five minutes of the drive, Tasha plotted Griffin's murder in grisly detail. Because she was in her final year of law school, most of the discussion was about how to get away with it. Eventually, she had Sydney laughing so hard she was crying. And then just crying.

When she finally looked up, they were in the parking lot of a strip mall. Tasha had killed the engine and was frantically digging through the car's glove compartment for a tissue. Finally, she held out an old napkin.

"I really can kill him," Tasha offered.

Sydney blew her nose. "That won't be necessary."

Tasha looked down at the dash and swallowed visibly. "I've never seen you cry before."

"I don't know that anyone has." Sydney stared down at the mangled strap of her purse. She thought about saying more about Griffin—because she'd cried in front him, but that had been right after they'd had sex and she didn't really think he'd noticed. That should have been a sign right there. But her throat closed over the words. So instead she said, "I don't know what I'm going to do about my job."

"You know he can't get away with that crap. He can't fire you over any of this. We'll sue his ass. We'll—"

"I don't... I know I could totally sue him. And maybe I should. For justice or whatever. But I don't really think that he'll fire me. He'll come to his senses and realize he can't get away with it. But I don't think I can go back to work there anyway. I can't see him every day."

"You could—"

But she shook her head. "Even if I found another position in the company, I'd still know I was working for him. I don't want that."

And here it was, reason number one why sleeping with her boss was a bad idea.

For a few long seconds, she was painfully aware of Tasha studying her. Then Tasha said fiercely, "You'll get another job!"

"In this economy?" Sydney shook her head. "It could take months. Yeah, I have my savings, but—" She broke off because her savings weren't all that extensive. She'd helped three of her four foster-siblings with college tuition, but the last thing she wanted was for Tasha to feel badly. "Hey, I can put the house on the market. I'll need to find an apartment that allows cats, but Grommet and I don't need all that room. It's a great little place in a great neighborhood. I'm sure I can—"

She broke off again, this time because Tasha was chuckling.

"What?" Sydney demanded.

"I'm not going to let you sell your house!"

"But—"

"God, you're so stubborn."

"I am not."

"Of course you are." Tasha twisted in her seat. "Look, you've helped with my tuition for the past four years. I'm not going to let you sell your house."

"I didn't help that much," she protested. She'd just chipped in here and there.

"You helped enough. I can get out of my apartment lease and move in with you. We'll share the mortgage payment. We could even get by with one car if we had to. And I've still got my job at the law library. We'll make it work. You're my sister. I'm not going to let you lose your home without a fight."

Tasha's words should have made her feel better, but they only made her cry more. It turned out she had a financial safety net after all. It was just her emotions that were free falling.

Griffin had ripped all of her long-sought-after security right out from under her. Her entire adult life, she'd worked to become financially independent. She'd struggled and scraped and starved to get where she was now…or rather, where she'd been a week ago. And because she'd slept with Griffin, she'd lost it all.

She should be devastated. She should be curling into a ball on the ground in tears. And she was devastated…just not about that. The job, the money, the security. She could live without all that. So she'd have to start over. Big deal. She could do that. Even without the safety net of family to help support her through the tough times, she'd still be fine.

No, what devastated her was that she'd lost Griffin. True, she'd never really had him. Her brain had never believed they'd get to be together, but somehow, despite that, her heart had believed it. Her heart had wanted and dreamed of what her brain had never dared to imagine: a life with Griffin. Her heart would have been happy in Houston, working for Cain Enterprises, or in sub-Saharan Africa. She would have gone anywhere to be with him. Unfortunately, he didn't want or need her.

She'd get over losing her job, but she might never recover from losing him.

In the end, Tasha didn't need to move in with her. The grueling search for a new job ended up being neither grueling nor long. The day after her big fight with Griffin, she'd resigned from Cain Enterprises. At first, he refused to even accept her resignation. He even went so far as to offer her a stiff apology. She didn't wait around to hear him out, but had left her letter on her desk on the way out. Four days after that, she got a call at home from Sheppard Capital. Sharlene offered her a job.

At first, Sydney was tempted to refuse. It smacked of charity. She didn't want a pity job merely because Griffin felt badly about giving her no option but to quit.

"Don't be ridiculous, dear," Sharlene had said, brushing aside her protests. "Griffin didn't call me. Dalton did. He was furious that Griffin put you in this position. Even in the heat of an argument, he should have known better. Dalton wanted to hire you himself, but he doesn't start with the new company for another three weeks, so I insisted I get first dibs. After all, I know how hard a good assistant is to come by. Besides, I also know what it means to be a man's assistant. To spend your every waking moment anticipating his needs only to find out he doesn't need you at all."

In the end, she had let Sharlene convince her. Not because she really wanted the job, but because it was easier than fighting her. Besides, she did need a job. The pay was nearly what she'd made at Cain Enterprises, and it was nice to go to work somewhere where no one knew that splotchy skin and red eyes weren't normal for her.

Sharlene's own assistant, apparently, had been wanting to move to their office in Dallas and so, after a week of unemployment, Sydney started work as Sharlene's new assistant.

A full week passed while she settled numbly into her new job. It was midway through her second week at the new job when Griffin walked into the office.

Seeing him at work was the one thing she hadn't anticipated when she'd accepted the job from Sharlene. The sight of him was like a kick to the solar plexus.

It took every ounce of willpower she had to swallow back her tears, muster her professionalism and ask politely, "Is Ms. Sheppard expecting you?"

Griffin looked her up and down without a trace of his normal easy smile. "No," he said simply. "I'm not here to see her."

That gave her a moment's pause. She hoped to hell that he was in the wrong office then because she just did not have the energy to be polite to him when all she really wanted to do was curl into a ball and cry. For about a month. Or even two.

Still, she kept a smile on her face that was at least semi-polite and asked, "Then can I direct you to someone else's office?"

"No. I'm right where I want to be." Before she ask what he meant, he pulled a business card down on the desk in front of her. "There. Will that do it?"

"What?"

"Look at the card, damn it."

His voice was hard and intractable. His face humorless.

She looked from him down to the business card. It had the familiar Cain Enterprises logo on the left-hand side. To the right of that were the words: Griffin Cain. And beneath that: President & Chief Executive Officer.

She stared at the card for a long moment before looking back up at him. "I don't understand."

"I've been working nonstop for the past two and half weeks to convince the board to name me CEO. Permanently. I groveled before my father. I called in all kinds of favors for this. I'm not quitting. I'm not leaving Cain Enterprises." With that, he walked around to her side of the desk and pulled her to her feet.

Then, before she could question him or protest, he dropped to one knee in front of her. He pulled out a ring box and flipped it open. Inside was a simple diamond solitaire. "Now, will you please marry me?"

The sight of him on his knees before her, the sight of the ring, the entire proposal…it was straight out of a fairy tale. And it killed her to have to turn him down.

"Griffin, I…" She started to shake her head, but she could barely talk past the tears.

He must have heard the denial in her voice because he stood, pulling her into his arms and cupping her face. "Don't say no."

"I can't…I can't say yes."

"Why not?"

His expression nearly broke her heart. Because he looked like he genuinely didn't know why she might say no.

She shook her head and pulled out of his arms. "Griffin, you don't really care about me."

To her surprise, he laughed. "That's ridiculous. Of course I do. I love you."

Her heart felt like it was trying to crawl right out of her and throw itself into his waiting hands. "You don't."

He grabbed her arm and pulled her back to him. "I do. I know you think you know me pretty well, but you don't get to tell me how I feel."

She swallowed her heart back down. She couldn't meet his gaze, so instead, she stared at the top button of his shirt. "You don't really mean that."

"I do."

"No. You don't. Look, I get why you might think you love me. But you really don't. It's just good sex and familiarity."

"It's great sex." He tipped her chin up so she was looking at him. "And it's love."

She forced herself to meet his gaze. "No. It's not." His arms felt so damn good around her and the sensation made it even harder to say what she had to say, but she forced the words out. "Things have been very complicated for you the past few weeks. You're confused. If you think you love me, it's just because I'm the one stable thing in your life right now and—"

Griffin interrupted her with a bark of laughter. "You think you're the one stable thing in my life?"

"Well, I—"

"Sydney, you make me crazy. You are maddening and delightful and you make me feel things no one else has ever made me feel. You tempt me beyond reason. The one thing you are not is stable."

"I—"

"You've driven me crazy ever since I first met you. Don't get me wrong, you are right about a lot of things, and you were totally right about me needing to stay on as CEO. But you are not right about why I'm asking you to marry me."

"I'm not?"

"I'm not asking you because I want stability in my life. I'm asking because I want you in my life."

"But...you don't really love me."

"What on earth makes you think I don't love you?"

"If you love me," she challenged, "why didn't you ever tell me about Hope2O?"

"If you love me why didn't you ever tell me about Sinnamon?"

For a moment, she stared at him, openmouthed. And then she realized she didn't have an answer for that.

Slowly, he smiled. "Hey, we both kept our secrets longer than we should have. We're both really private people. This crazy search for the heiress did turn everything upside down. But that's not a bad thing. If this hadn't happened, we probably would have taken a lot longer to get here. But I don't have any doubt that we still would have gotten here. I love you, Sydney. I think I've loved you ever since we first met. And if that doesn't convince you, then consider this. I spent the past two weeks flying all over the country, meeting with each member of the board to convince them to name me CEO. All so that I could make this proposal perfect. I messed up the first time I asked you to marry me. I wanted to do it right this time."

Again, he dropped to his knee in front of her and held out the ring box.

"Sydney Edwards, will you marry me?"

And suddenly, she was crying again. She, who never cried in front of anyone and would have sworn she was cried out for the rest of her life, was crying. So she never actually said yes. She just nodded until he got the hint. He stood up and kissed her through her tears.

Finally, a long time later, she looked up, smiling a little. "I don't suppose this is a good time to give you back that key to your condo."

He frowned, and it seemed to take him a moment to realize what she meant. Then he chuckled. "No. Why don't you keep that? It might come in handy when we're planning the wedding."

She pushed up on her toes and was about to kiss him again when she realized he was wearing a sweater. The same cashmere sweater she had him wear to that first board meeting. "You're wearing Dalton's sweater," she said softly.

"You said I looked good in it. So I made him give it to me. He was happy to donate to the cause. He said he'd give up all his sweaters if I'd just stop moping and come after you."

She gave his arm a playful punch. "You weren't really moping, were you? You're not the type to mope."

He smiled. "Not anymore, I'm not."

Epilogue

"Now we know. This is the girl we're looking for," Griffin said.

Sydney walked back into Griffin's living room carrying a tray of coffee mugs just in time to see him carefully place the two photos on the ottoman in front of his sectional sofa. Sydney set the tray of coffee on the end table. Griffin reached for his mug immediately, sending her a grateful smile as he did.

She felt that familiar little flutter in her heart as she returned his smile. How had she gotten so lucky?

Before she could distribute the rest of the coffees, Dalton handed one to Laney, who sat on the sofa beside him. Laney gave Dalton's leg a squeeze as she took the coffee from him, but instead of drinking it herself, she carried it over to the window where Cooper stood looking out.

Sydney had met Cooper only that morning, at Laney and Dalton's wedding. The event had been a quiet affair, done in the backyard of the Cain estate, so that Hollister's nurse could wheel him out to watch.

For now, because all three brothers were in town for the wedding, Griffin had called this meeting. He'd seemed relived that Cooper had shown up. Laney handed Cooper his coffee, giving his arm a friendly rub. He smiled down at her with more affection than he'd shown either of his brothers.

Laney returned to her spot beside Dalton, curling her feet under her as she sat. Cooper wandered over, sipping his coffee as he looked down at the pictures.

"You haven't exactly been making lightning-fast progress, have you?"

Griffin shot him an annoyed look. "I've been a little busy running the company."

A little busy was putting it mildly. Griffin had attacked the position as CEO with the same fervor he dedicated to all his projects. Hope2O wasn't suffering from neglect, either. Now that the cat was out of the bag, Sharlene had joined Hope2O's board and together they were plotting to get Dalton involved. Between the three of them, they would take good care of the charity.

Sydney ran her palm across his leg and she felt some of the tension seep out of him before Griffin added, "But, no, not particularly. Hollister's condition has stabilized, but we can't put this off forever."

"Griffin is right," Dalton said. "We've got to find this girl."

Cooper looked at them all with a raised eyebrow. "Based on nothing more than a pair of old photographs?"

Sydney scooted to the edge of the seat and reached over to turn the photos so they faced Cooper. By now, she figured she knew as much as any of them, maybe more. "We know this is the girl." She pointed to the child in the picture. "This was taken years ago, obviously. We figure she's about Griffin's age now. This woman here was her mother. When she worked for the Cains she used the name Vivian Beck, but we don't think that's her real name."

"Why?" Cooper asked.

"Because she disappeared after she was fired," Griffin explained. "We tried to track her down by social security number, but that was a dead end, too."

Dalton stared at the picture. "So we still have nothing."

"Not exactly." Sydney took another sip of her coffee. "When we showed the picture to Hollister, he called the mother Vee, not Vivian. And he admitted that when she came to Houston and got the job as the Cain nanny, she had followed him from somewhere. In a later conversation, he called her Victoria. So I looked up the company records to see where he'd been in the months before she got that job and found out that he'd just returned from—"

"Victoria," Dalton said.

Sydney looked up at him, but he and Laney were exchanging a look.

"So I was right," Laney said. "Victoria was the name of the girl's mother, in addition to being the name of a city."

Dalton nodded, his expression grim. "So that's what we know. In 1982 Hollister spent three months in Victoria, Texas. And while he was there, he met and—presumably impregnated—a young woman whose name was also Victoria. So it shouldn't be too hard to track her down. How many women named Victoria could there possibly be in Victoria, Texas?"

"Exactly," Griffin said. "Once we find the mother, we should be able to track down the daughter."

Cooper frowned. "You're sure this is the woman who wrote the letter?"

Sydney shot a sidelong look at Griffin. He'd gone back and forth on whether or not he wanted to tell his brothers that Caro had written the letter. She took his hand in hers and gave it a squeeze.

"Yes," he lied as he tapped his finger on the photo of the girl. "I'm sure this girl here is the one we're looking for."

"Well, then." Cooper took one last sip of his coffee before

tting his mug on the table. "It seems like you've got this all
rapped up. It seems like you've won."

Griffin stood before Cooper could walk out. "I didn't ask
ou to come just so I could rub your nose in it."

"Then why did you ask me here?"

"Neither Dalton nor I have been able to find this girl on our
wn. We're all tired of Hollister's games. I think we should
ork together—we need your help. I think we should split
e money."

"You want to divide up the company three ways?"

"No. Four ways. Once we find her, we give her a quarter of
. After all, she's our sister."

* * * * *